HOCKEY WARS 4

CHAMPIONSHIPS

SAM LAWRENCE & BEN JACKSON

ILLUSTRATOR DANKO HERRERA

www.indiepublishinggroup.com

ISBN: 978-1-988656-34-2 Paperback

ISBN: 978-1-988656-35-9 Hardcover

Editor: Bobbi Beatty

Winning the state championship, that represented your neighborhood. I would have to say that it was my biggest thrill ever. It was just the guys in the neighborhood and that was special.

—*Herb Brooks*

OTHER BOOKS BY SAM & BEN

Hockey Wars Series

Hockey Wars

Hockey Wars 2 - The New Girl

Hockey Wars 3 - The Tournament

Hockey Wars 4 - Championships

Hockey Wars 5 - Lacrosse Wars (Coming Spring 2020)

My Little Series

The Day My Fart Followed Me Home

The Day My Fart Followed Me To Hockey

The Day My Fart Followed Santa Up The Chimney

The Day My Fart Followed Me To Soccer

The Day My Fart Followed Me To The Dentist

The Day My Fart Followed Me To The Zoo

The Day My Fart Followed Me To Baseball

It's Not Easy Being A Little Fart

If I Was A Caterpillar

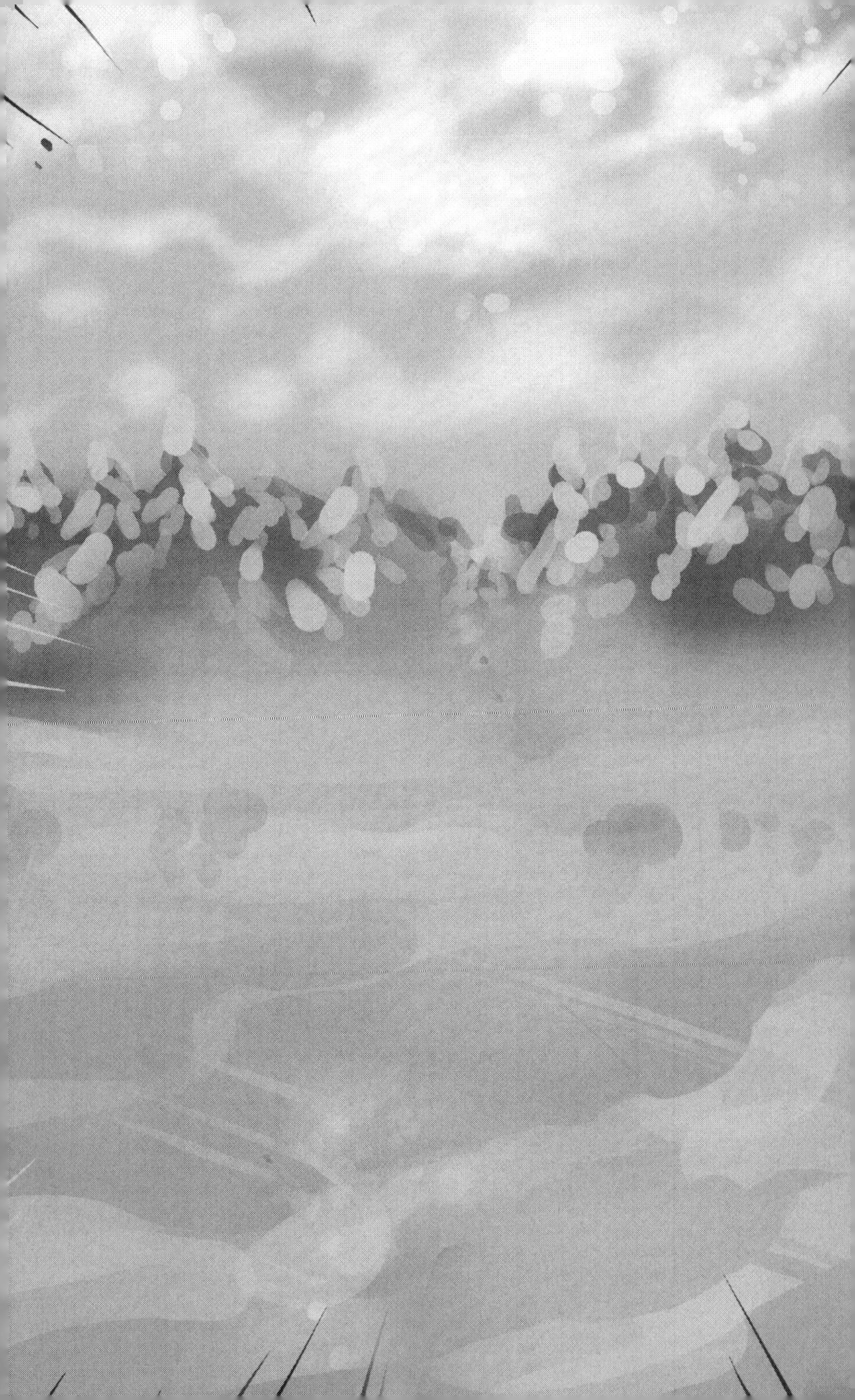

1

IT HAD BEEN three weeks since the boys and girls of the Dakota Lightning and Hurricanes hockey teams took the win in their first away tournament, and both teams were still celebrating.

The only problem was that one of the boys' senior players, Linkin, had broken his arm, and the rest of the boys' team was nervously awaiting the news from his doctor about whether or not he'd be able to play again for the rest of the season.

The boys were out on the field playing their own version of soccer. Snow soccer. It had the same rules as regular soccer, except you played it in the snow and got a whole lot wetter, dirtier, and colder than regular soccer.

"Those boys are going to be so messy," Mia said to the other girls gathered around her as they

sat on one of the hard wooden benches looking across the white field. Every now and again, a cold gust of wind would send flurries of snow whipping across the field. That didn't seem to slow down the boys, who, despite their winter boots and coats, were slipping and sliding in the muddy snow as they tried to kick the soccer ball around the field.

Mia's boyfriend, Cameron, was the captain of the boys' team. He also happened to be Millie's best friend. This had caused quite a lot of drama when Mia had first arrived in Dakota and even more drama at their recent tournament when Millie had become friends with Liam, a boy from the Blue Devils, Cameron's opposition.

"Please. When aren't they? I swear, they could give sports a bit of a rest for five minutes." Millie answered.

"I don't know; it does look like mega fun. You know?" Khloe said, wistfully looking out at the boys running around like crazy on the white snow-covered field. This comment earned Khloe a dirty look from several of the girls, but she didn't care. She would have been just as happy out there kicking the soccer ball around in the snow and mud as any of the boys.

"Speaking of boys, who's the new guy you were

talking to at the tournament, Mills?" Violet asked. This was followed by a large chorus of "oohs" as all the girls crammed in, surrounding Millie to get the gossip.

"No one, really. We're just friends," Millie answered, blushing and turning bright red, her face burning. *Stupid face*, she thought to herself, *always giving me away*.

Just as they had all settled into class, Linkin arrived, looking glum, with his arm in a bright blue cast.

"Linkin! What happened to your other cast?" Cameron asked, jumping up to help Linkin with his school bag.

"The specialist changed it today. Apparently, my arm wasn't healing as fast as they had expected it to. She said the break was a little more complicated than they had first thought."

"Dude! Are you serious right now?" Rhys shouted dramatically from the back of the classroom as he threw his hands up in the air.

"Excuse me, Rhys? I'll have you remember where you are. This isn't a hockey arena!" Their teacher said crossly, looking down her nose at Rhys, her metal-framed glasses perched carefully on the tip of her nose.

Rhys knew better than to try and argue with Mrs. Rice, who all the kids affectionately called Mrs. C because her first name was Connie.

"Sorry, Mrs. C," Rhys said quietly, causing some of the other kids to snicker until a quick look from their teacher stopped them dead in their tracks.

"So, how long until you're able to play?" Cameron asked Linkin as the two of them sat down at their desks.

"Well, the specialist said I wouldn't be able to play again this season. By the time I get my cast off and finish doing physiotherapy, it's going to be too late to play."

"Man, that sucks. We really need you."

"Sorry, guys. Once I get the cast removed in a few weeks, I can start doing light training with you guys, but no contact. And really, the season will be over then," Linkin said sadly.

"It's all good. We—" Cameron started to say before he was abruptly interrupted by their teacher.

"Boys. Now I appreciate you have some news to catch up on, but it's going to have to wait until lunchtime. Cameron, I know you haven't done nearly as much on your project as you should have, and, Linkin, you haven't even started. So, let's get on with it, shall we?" Mrs. C said sternly to the two chattering boys.

"Yes, Mrs. C!" The two boys said quickly, turning their attention to their project.

The remainder of the class went by fast as all the kids got on with their work, and it wasn't long before the bell sounded to signal lunchtime. In a few minutes, the class had emptied completely as they all streamed out to eat their lunches in their favorite spots.

All the hockey boys and girls headed to their favorite benches near the cafeteria. They had important business to discuss.

"So, as you all know, after all the cold weather we *finally* had, the pond is going to be open this weekend." This news by Millie, the captain of the girl's team, brought a chorus of cheers, clapping, and whistles from the kids gathered around her. They had all been eagerly awaiting the opening of the pond, which had been really delayed because of the mild winter. "Now, we all know arguing over who plays on the pond and when isn't going to work out well for anyone, so let's mix it up this weekend."

"What happened last time?" Mia whispered to Cameron. Mia was the newest girl on the team, so she hadn't been around last winter.

"We got into a big argument, and it turned into a feud," Cameron whispered back. Mia rolled her eyes. Trust Cam and Millie to turn a frozen pond into a feud.

"I was thinking, and Cameron agreed, that we could play mixed teams on the pond this weekend. We're all going to be really busy the next few weekends getting ready for the championships, so this might be the last time we can all get together before the pond melts," Millie added, trying to put a positive spin on her plan. Both she and Cameron knew that if the two captains were on board, the rest of the teams would be okay with it, and there wouldn't be any grumbling.

"How are we picking teams?" Khloe asked.

"Well, we were thinking we'd pick them, but with a twist. We'll alternate picks between girls and boys so all the picks are even. Does that sound cool?" Cameron asked the two groups. The news was greeted to nods and claps.

"Cool by me."

"Sounds awesome."

"Okay, well, if everyone agrees, then we'll meet at the pond to pick teams. Same deal as usual. If you show up with your gear, you'll get a game. If you're not there, you'll miss out. Now that we have that sorted out, who's keen for some snow soccer?" Cameron shouted, walking outside and kicking the soccer ball as far out onto the field as he could before sprinting hard after it.

Most of the boys and a few girls streamed out onto the field after the ball, while the rest of the kids settled down to talk about the upcoming championship, pond hockey, and who was dating who.

2

ALL THE BOYS were sitting around, getting ready in the change room with the usual chatter and horseplay when the conversation veered toward how they were going to replace Linkin in the upcoming championship in a few weeks.

"Do you know what we're going to do about Linkin yet, Cam?" Hunter asked as they sat tying their skates. The two of them had been best friends for as long as either could remember, both having played hockey on the same team together for years.

"I don't know. We have a couple options, but I still wish Linkin was playing with us."

"Maybe we could just play with one less player?" Hunter chimed in.

"No way! Coach John would never do that," Rhys added.

"What other choice do we have?" Cameron said, "the only player that's any good from the other two teams is..." Cameron trailed off as the change room door opened, and Coach John walked in with a player from one of the other teams.

"Boys, I'd like you to all say hello to—" Coach John started to say.

"Riley! What are you doing here?" Rhys blurted out.

"Riley is going to be coming up and playing with us in the championships. His team has playoffs next weekend, but they didn't make it to championships."

"Are you kidding me? No way!" Rhys said, throwing his hands in the air. "Coach! I—"

"Rhys, this isn't up for discussion. Your little brother was nice enough to come and help us out, so I don't want to hear any more about it."

"Don't worry, Rhys. I won't tell everyone how much you suck," Riley said, sticking out his tongue. "I'll just show them out on the ice!" The rest of the boys all laughed, enjoying seeing Rhys on the receiving end for once. Usually, Rhys was teasing one of them.

Cameron looked up at the ceiling, slowing shaking his head, hoping it would somehow open up and save him from this terrible situation developing right in front of him. Cameron had been friends with Rhys long enough to know that both he and Riley were super competitive when it came to anything, especially hockey. This was not going to end very well unless they could find a way to play together.

"Dude, I don't care what anyone says, I don't think I'm ever going to love practice," Rhys grumbled as he brushed some ice off the side of his leg.

"You're not supposed to love it, Rhys; you're supposed to be learning something!" Coach John shouted across the ice.

"I swear, his hearing seems to be getting better every year," Rhys said, rolling his eyes. Cameron tried his best, but he couldn't help but laugh at what his friend had just said. Encouraged, Rhys continued.

"I mean, aren't old people supposed to lose their hearing as they get older? His seems to be getting sharper each year."

"Rhys! Have you ever thought it could just be

that your mouth is getting bigger?" Coach John shouted again from where he was talking with some of the assistant coaches. "But I'm glad you spoke up because we were just talking about who was going to volunteer to stay behind and help clean the change room. Thanks!"

"Oh, man!" Rhys moaned. *When would he learn to keep his big mouth shut?*

"It's not his fault, Coach; his mouth does a lot of his thinking for him." Riley said as he lined up on the other side of the ice, ready to continue their drill.

Rhys didn't bother replying; he'd let his stick do the talking.

Coach John flicked the puck out to the center of the ice, and both brothers took off from opposite sides, heading for the puck sliding toward them. Neither of them was willing to give an inch, and they both slammed together, crashing down on the ice hard.

"Rhys! Riley! Enough. If you two can't learn to play as teammates, then neither of you is going to play, and I'll find two other kids who *are* willing to work together. Now, go up the other end of the arena and show everyone how good you are at doing push-ups."

"How many, Coach?" Riley asked.

"Until I get tired of watching you." This comment earned a chorus of laughter from the other boys until the coach swung around and silenced them all with a look. None of them wanted to end up doing push-ups with the two brothers and knew it was time to shush up.

The rest of the practice ran smoothly, with both Riley and Rhys managing to stay away from each other and avoiding the wrath of Coach John and any more push-ups.

Cameron, Millie, and Mia were sitting in the foyer of the arena, chatting while they waited for Cameron's mom to pick them up.

"What was Coach John thinking?" Millie said, shaking her head.

"Why? What happened?" Mia asked. She had only moved to town at the end of the last season and hadn't grown up together with the others as Cam and Millie had.

"Coach John got Riley, Rhys' younger brother, to play with us for the championships," Cameron said. "He's going to be filling in for Linkin."

"So, what's the problem with that? If he's good enough to play, you should be happy to have him." Mia replied. She couldn't see any problem with another player helping the boys out, even if it was someone's little brother.

"Oh, don't get me wrong, we're lucky to have him. He's a great player, but there's one problem."

"He's a miniature Rhys!" Millie said, interrupting Cam.

"Oh, I think I see the problem now!" Mia said, laughing.

"Yep. They both have a big mouth and a short fuse. If they can't learn to play together as teammates, then they could end up causing more problems for us. We don't need the drama heading into the championships," Cam added.

Going into any game with a new player was a big ask for any team, but adding a family feud into the mix could end up being a nightmare for the boys. If those two couldn't get their act together, it was going to be the shortest run at a championship ever.

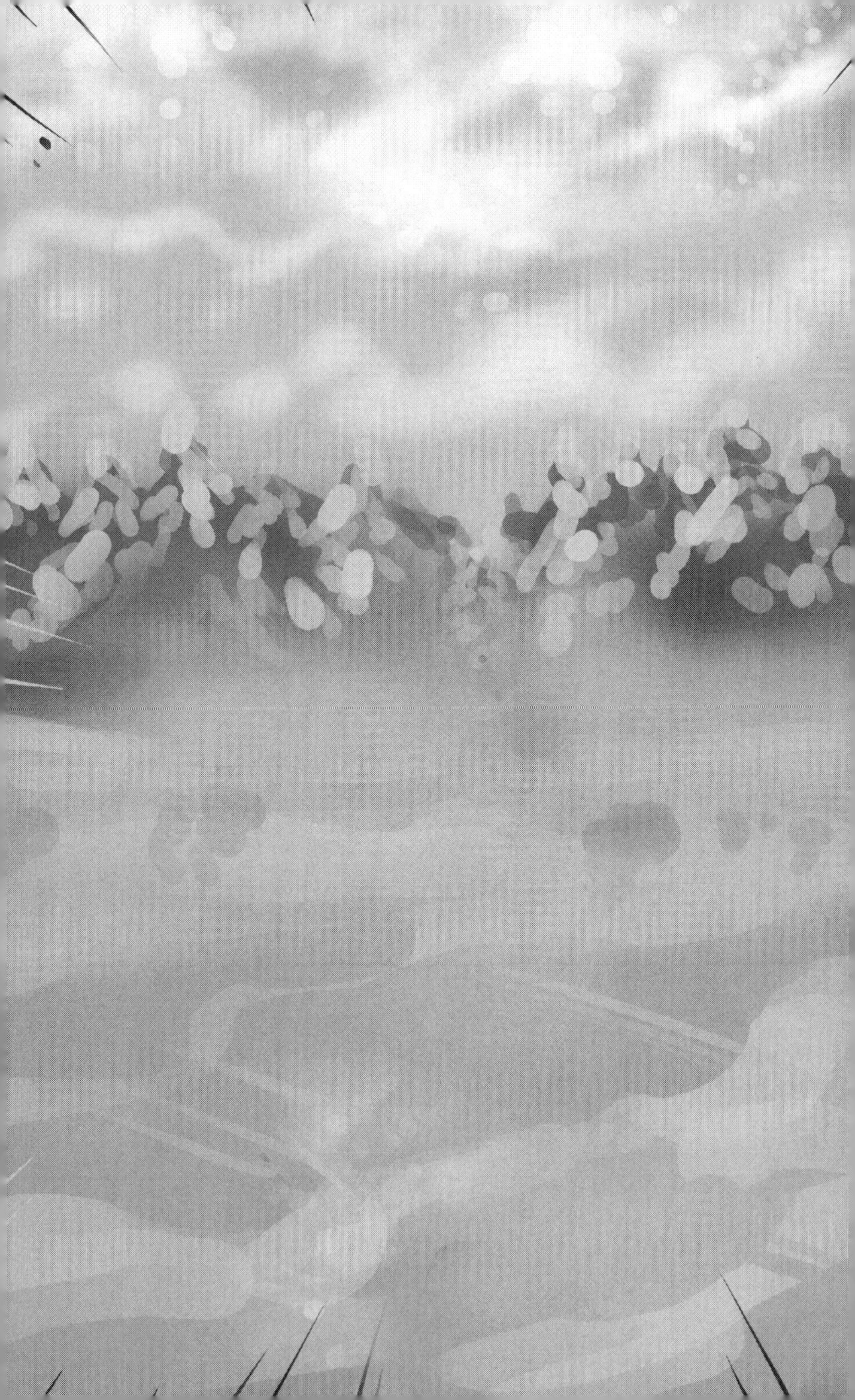

3

MILLIE, GEORGIA, AND Mia were up late discussing how they could earn money to help offset the costs of the upcoming championships. Even though Mia was relatively new to town and the team, she had soon become best friends with both Millie and Georgia, turning the regular duo into a terrific trio.

Though all the kids payed team fees to play and sponsors donated some money, there were still a lot of out-of-pocket costs associated with hockey championships and tournaments. This meant it was up to both teams to organize fundraisers to help ease some of the costs.

The boys' team put a lot of energy into shoveling snow from people's driveways and sidewalks to help raise money, but the girls had a much more appealing idea.

"OMG! I have it!" Mia shouted, interrupting the quiet as all three girls sat trying to figure out their own fundraising idea in Millie's bedroom.

"Shh! You'll wake up my parents!" Millie hissed, clamping her hand over Mia's mouth.

"Oops. Sorry," Mia said, giggling.

"What's your idea?" Georgia asked.

"Well, at my last school, to help with fundraising, we sold candygrams," Mia explained.

"What are candygrams?" Millie asked. She'd never heard of anything like it before.

"They're like messages, but with candy. Instead of just giving someone a Valentine's card, they come to us, and we deliver their message with candy. We charged a dollar per candygram. We'll dress up, and all the girls can run around the school delivering them. We made a bundle doing it."

"It definitely sounds like heaps more fun than shoveling snow all day," Georgia said. She wasn't exactly known for doing manual labor, and dressing up and delivering Valentine's Day messages was something she thought she would love doing.

Millie agreed. "Okay, Mia, I think it's a great idea. We need to get permission from Coach Phil first and then ask Mr. Potter if the school will approve this since we're going to do it at school. After that, we should be good to start getting it all sorted out."

As it was well past when the three girls should have been sleeping, they wrapped up the unofficial team meeting and got ready for bed. Despite the late hour, the girls were all restless, and it ended up being another hour or more before they finally drifted off to sleep.

Most of both teams showed up ready to play on the pond on Saturday. The weather had turned out great, and they were able to clear off the ice with their makeshift shovel Zambonis. The pond ice wasn't strong enough to support a real Zamboni, so the kids made do with what they had.

The two captains took turns picking their players until everyone had a spot on one of the teams. There was a lot of laughter and drama as people were picked, but no one's feelings were hurt, and they all knew they would get an opportunity to play.

Linkin couldn't play, but that hadn't stopped him from showing up in a ref uniform to join in.

"Dude! Nice ref gear!" Preston shouted at Linkin, sliding up to him and spraying him with ice and snow. Linkin didn't respond straight away. Instead, he turned slowly, pulled a whistle out of his jacket, and blew it loudly, throwing his hand up dramatically at the same time.

"Number thirty-three, unsportsmanlike conduct. Two minutes!"

"Linkin! Are you serious? I thought we were buddies?"

"I'll thank you to call me ref, sir," Linkin replied, doing his best English accent, "and any more lip out of you, and I'll have you benched for the rest of the game!"

Well, this started the rest of the kids laughing, with half the players rolling around on the ice and snow laughing hysterically.

Eventually, the game got started again, and both teams took their best shots on each other. They had already agreed there would be no contact. Neither team could afford to take an injury into the championships, especially the boys, who were already down one player.

The changes coming off the bench wouldn't

have impressed either teams' coach. Most of the kids were busy trying to take selfies, which wasn't easy when you were wearing hockey gloves.

"Seriously?! There are like two of us out there! How about you put your phones away and hit the ice, slackers?" Rhys said as he slid into the section that had been allocated as his team's bench, knocking kids left and right. "We're getting slaughtered out there!"

"Rhys!" Millie shouted.

"What, Mills?"

"Smile!" Millie replied, leaning in for a selfie. When she checked the photo, it showed a furious Rhys and Millie beaming the cutest smile she could. Khloe throwing up bunny ears behind Rhys' head made the photo even funnier.

While the kids played hockey out on the pond, a few of the parents had shown up to have their own fun. One of the dads had brought a load of firewood down, and there was a roaring fire going in the large fire pit.

With the fire roaring and the sun setting, the kids slowly made their way off the ice and headed toward the warm glow of the large fire. Millie's and Cameron's moms had brought hot chocolate, and another parent broke out bags of fluffy marshmallows and passed them around the growing circle of kids.

It wasn't long before the wind started to pick up, and a chill blew through the woods surrounding the pond, signaling it was time for everyone to pack up and head home for the night.

"I'm going to walk Mia home, Mom," Cameron said, throwing his hockey equipment in the back of his mom's car and picking up Mia's bag, slinging it over his shoulder.

"Okay, but don't hang around too long. I think there's more snow forecast for tonight."

"Thanks, Cam. I would have been fine, though." Mia said as they walked away.

"No worries. It's the least I can do. How'd you enjoy the game?"

"It's awesome playing on the pond. I think I like the hot chocolate and toasted marshmallows afterward even more than hockey, though!" Mia replied, laughing.

The two of them soon covered the distance to Mia's house, and Cameron walked up to the porch to say goodnight. Mia's mom had heard the two kids coming up the sidewalk and flicked the porch light on for them.

"Thanks for seeing Mia home, Cameron. It was very nice of you." Mia's mom said, grabbing the hockey bag and dropping it into the mudroom. *The two of them are adorable*; she thought to herself as Cameron stood awkwardly on the porch.

"That's okay. It was nothing," Cameron said, blushing.

"I'll text you later, Cam," Mia said, waving goodbye to her boyfriend as he walked down the twisting sidewalk toward the road and home.

As soon as Millie walked into her house, it started to ding with messages from Liam.

Liam was curious about how the pond hockey game had gone, and Millie had lots of photos to send him from all the selfies they'd all been taking on the bench.

Where Liam lived, they weren't lucky enough to have a pond, so they had to settle for backyard ice rinks some of the parents made.

Millie also filled Liam in on their plan to raise money for the championships by sending candygrams on Valentine's Day. If all went well, they would have enough extra money for the championships.

4

MILLIE HAD CALLED an impromptu meeting in the school cafeteria on Monday morning for the girls of the Hurricanes. Up for discussion was the idea to sell candygrams to raise money for the championships.

"Okay, girls. Mia, Georgia, and I came up with an idea for fundraising this year. Coach Phil and Mr. Potter have already given us the okay, so now it's time to start getting ready," Millie said, addressing the large group of girls.

"Well, what is it?" Khloe asked, cutting straight to the point as usual.

"Oh yeah," Millie said as she giggled. She hadn't told them all yet. "We're selling candygrams!"

"What on earth are candygrams?" Kiera, one of the junior players, asked.

"Mia? It's your idea, so you should explain it," Millie said, handing it over to her friend.

"Well, they're like regular Valentine's Day messages, but instead of people giving them to others themselves, we'll be delivering them for them. Along with a small bag of candy. We're going to dress up and charge a dollar per candygram." Mia explained.

Once Mia had explained to the team what they would be doing, there was a lot of excited talk about dressing up and how'd they deliver the messages. Everyone was super excited to be taking part, and it sure beat the usual bake sale they'd put on in the past.

"Okay, I'll make an announcement over the PA sometime today to let everyone know what we're doing, and we'll have a team meeting tonight at my house. I told my mom, and she said we could turn it into a pizza party, so you don't need to worry about dinner. If anyone can't make it, just text me, but you can all come over straight after school if you like." Now that Millie had told the team and gotten permission, they would all spend the night getting the candygrams ready.

It was all coming together nicely, Millie thought to herself. With a bit of luck, they'd be able to raise plenty of money for their championships week.

HAPPY
DAY

The kids were all eating in the cafeteria when the loudspeakers blared to life, cutting through the noise of the kids talking, eating, and laughing.

"Attention! Sorry to interrupt lunch. This Valentine's Day, the Hurricanes will be selling candygrams to raise money for our championships. If you'd like to send your friends or your crush a message, just come see us at the table at the end of the cafeteria. We'll be selling them each break until Thursday. They're only a dollar each, but don't leave it too late, or you'll miss out! Thanks!"

Millie's announcement over the loudspeaker sparked a lot of chatter as all the kids in the cafeteria started to talk to their friends about who they would send a candygram to.

"Was that Millie?" Hunter asked Cameron and some of the other boys sitting at his lunch table.

"Yeah, I knew they weren't doing their usual bake sale this year, but Mia was keeping it a secret from me until they made the announcement," Cameron replied.

"When are we starting the snow shoveling?" Rhys asked.

"Umm, I think the coach has a list ready for us to start on tonight and tomorrow."

"Man, I know we make a lot of money shoveling, but I do not appreciate the early mornings before school," Linkin said.

"Who are you kidding? How much snow will you be shoveling with a broken arm?" Rhys replied.

"That's true. However, when I raised that exact point with the coach, he said I'd be able to carry a shovel one-handed just as well as anyone else," Linkin said, shaking his head.

"Sucked in!" Rhys said, laughing. All the other boys joined in and laughed too. It looked like no one would miss out on the fun job of shoveling snow in the cold before school. Even Linkin.

"Okay, everyone, listen up!" Georgia shouted across Millie's living room, shushing everyone up so Millie could get them started on their project.

"Thanks, Georgia. We have all the Valentine's Day cards in a big pile over there. We need to punch a hole in the corner of each one. There are some heart-shaped hole punches sitting on the table. After that, we need to divide the candy into the small bags and tie one card to each bag."

"Are we writing anything in them now, Millie?" Khloe asked.

"No, each card already has a message in them. Customers will write the names in when they order them at school, or they can add their own message in them if they prefer. But I guess we could charge double if they want us to write a message," Mia answered.

"Thanks, Mia. That's a good way to make some extra money! Okay, so everyone divides up into groups, and we'll get these all done. Mom's ordering a whole bunch of different pizzas, so we'll take a break to eat and then finish off whatever's left after dinner. Is anyone allergic to anything?" Millie asked.

"Umm, I'm allergic to peanuts," one of the juniors, Aniyah, replied, "but pizza is normally okay."

"Okay, I'll let Mom know just in case."

"Thanks, Mills."

"No worries. Okay, everyone divide up, and let's get this candygram party started!" Millie shouted. It wouldn't take them long to finish the candygrams if they all worked together, and it gave the junior players a good chance to hang out with the senior players.

Even though they all played on the same team,

they still mostly hung out with the girls from their own age groups. Whenever they could get together and bond as a team, it helped them on the ice.

Two hours later, Millie's mom walked into her living room and called a dinner break. As she looked around the room, she noticed almost every flat surface was covered with either Valentine's Day cards, candy bags, ribbon, or other craft materials.

"Well, it does look as if you've all been extremely busy. Take a break and have some pizza. Aniyah, I checked with the pizza shop, and they assured me there are no peanuts or peanut allergy issues with any of the pizzas, so help yourself to whatever sort you like, honey." Millie's mom said to the group of girls.

"Thanks, Mrs....umm, Millie."

"Don't be silly. You can call me Patty, and that goes for the rest of you girls. Now, go and wash up and get some pizza before it all gets cold."

The girls all crowded into the large kitchen and helped themselves to pizza and garlic bread. There was plenty to go around, and it wasn't long before they all found themselves full to bursting. They helped Millie's mom clean up the pizza mess and headed back into the living room to finish their candygrams.

Just as they were cleaning up the last of the mess from the candygrams, Millie's mom walked in with some large posters she had designed for the girls. They would be able to put the posters up around the school to help them drum up some more sales.

Overall, it was a great night, with all the girls hanging out together and bonding as they made the candygrams. *Now all they had to do was sell them and then deliver them on Valentine's Day*, Millie thought to herself.

5

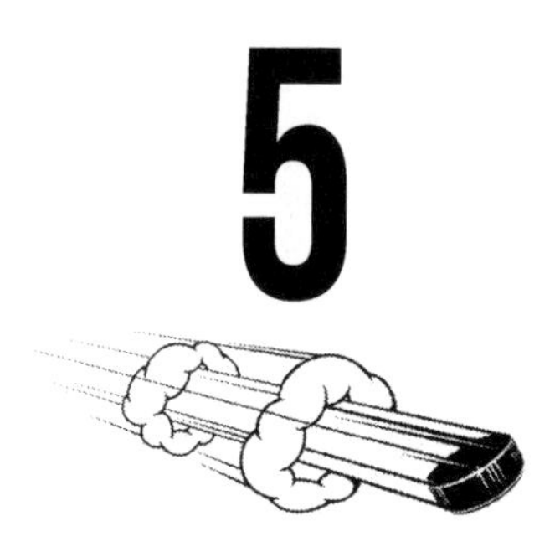

WITH PERMISSION TO set up and sell their candygrams, the girls took the opportunity to sneak out of class a few minutes early and set their table up near the cafeteria. This would give them the best chance of selling their candygrams as all the other kids headed to eat.

"So, how does it work?" one of the senior boys asked Millie, who was busy getting everything ready before the rush began.

"Well, it's super easy. You buy the candygram from us and write a message on the card if you want. Once you've done that, just seal it in the envelope and then put the name and class on the front. We'll deliver it for you on Valentine's Day. If you want us to write the message for you, then it will cost double."

"Okay, cool," The boy replied, looking at all the different cards on the table. "Do I need to write the message now, or can I drop it off later?"

"No, you can write it anytime during the week up until Thursday and just drop it in the box."

"Okay, awesome. I'll grab one, thanks." The senior said handing over a dollar.

"Thanks! First sale. Make sure you tell all your friends," Georgia said, grabbing the money and putting it in the money tin the girls had on the table.

By now, there was a long line of kids starting to gather at the table, all looking to grab a candygram before they ran out.

As it turned out, that wasn't a bad idea as the girls sold their entire stock of candygrams in the first lunch break. They hadn't expected them to be that popular and made plans to get together at one of the other girl's houses and get another batch ready to sell at school tomorrow.

"Come on, guys; if you can't get a simple drill right, we might as well not even show up at the championships. I know you're better than this. Now get it together!" Coach John shouted, shaking his head and rubbing his temples. It was going to be a long practice.

This practice was going about as well as the last practice, with Rhys and Riley still not able to work together. The problem was that it didn't just make them play badly; it was affecting the entire team.

"Rhys, you gotta let this go, man. It's starting to affect the rest of the team, and Coach John looks like he's about to blow a gasket," Cameron said as he slid into line behind Rhys. As the captain, it was his job to make sure all the players got along, and right now, Rhys and his little brother were causing some serious problems.

"Don't blame me! I tried, Cam, but he's doing everything he can to annoy me. The worst thing is some of the juniors love him, and they're starting to annoy me too just to impress him."

Just to emphasize his point, as Rhys took off on the next drill and tried to intercept the pass, one of the juniors flubbed the pass and made him miss it. This set off a round of laughter from all the juniors and Riley. The only person that wasn't laughing was Coach John. He threw his arms up in the air, sending his clipboard flying in the process.

Cameron was shaking his head too. It was going to be a long practice, and their chances of winning anything at the championships were getting slimmer and slimmer. *If only Linkin hadn't broken his arm*, Cameron thought to himself. Now, he had this drama to deal with.

If they didn't get their acts together, they'd never stand a chance.

Friday rolled around all too soon for the girls. Their candygrams had proven to be a massive success. They'd sold out twice more and raised several hundred dollars for the team's fundraising effort.

What had surprised the girls the most was that the teachers had bought a candygram for every child in their class. This way, no one missed out, and almost everyone was lucky enough to get two or three candygrams.

The girls had all dressed up like cupids and gotten permission to go from classroom to classroom, delivering the candygrams to the students. The principal had allowed the deliveries but made it a condition that no one was allowed to open the candygrams or eat their candy until recess.

When Millie walked back into her classroom, she was surprised to see there were three candygrams sitting on her desk.

170 - 30 - 16
7
π·r²
+500
+150
+30
÷4
920
a
h
b

"Did I forget some?" she asked Mia, surprised.

"No, silly, they're for you!" Mia replied quietly.

Millie couldn't help but blush when she scooped the candygrams up and read who they were from. She wasn't supposed to open them, but her curiosity had gotten the better of her.

There was one from Georgia, Cameron, and Liam. For the life of her, she couldn't work out how Liam had managed it. *Someone must have been helping him*, she thought. *But which one of her sneaky friends had it been?* Millie thought as she looked around the classroom.

Georgia was sitting over at her desk, trying to look innocent but putting in way too much effort. Any other time she would have already been pestering Millie to see what was going on.

"You!" Millie whispered at her friend, who was now giggling away, not even trying to pretend. "How did he do it?"

"Well, I was texting that boy we met at the tournament, Greyson, from the Blue Devils, and he asked about the candygrams. Apparently, you mentioned them to Liam, and Liam had asked Greyson to ask me to help get one for you."

"OMG. He's so cute!" Mia said, joining in on the whispered conversation.

"I know, right? How cute is it that he went to all that trouble to make sure he got you a candygram Mills?"

Millie just nodded and blushed. It so was cool that he'd gone to so much effort to get her a Valentine's Day card. Especially considering she hadn't expected it at all. Now the only problem was that she was so excited to get home so she could talk to Liam, the rest of the day was going to drag by and feel like a week.

6

EVEN THOUGH VALENTINE'S Day was last week, all the kids at school were still talking about how cool the candygrams had been. After they had paid for all their expenses, the girls had raised over three hundred dollars from the candygrams to help with the championships.

All that and they hadn't even had to shovel any snow! It had turned out to be a massive success.

There was only one weekend left before championships, but all the hockey kids had another event on their mind: Millie's birthday party.

They had all had a rough week on the ice, with both teams doing double training sessions twice this week. They'd also been surprised with an off-ice training session to review game tapes from the previous tournament games they had to sit through before they could even think about the party.

"Dude, you didn't tell me they were taping the last game. I would have tried one of my trademark dance moves," Rhys said to Cameron.

"We've all seen you dance, bro. You should be thankful no one told you they were taping," Logan said.

"He's right, Rhys. You're a terrible dancer. Now, pay attention—all of you—because I've been less than impressed with what I've seen over the last two weeks," Coach John demanded, interrupting their whispered conversation. "And while we're talking about on-ice performances, yours was less than impressive, Cameron. I'm not sure what was going on during that game with you and that other guy—"

"Liam, Millie's new boyfriend!" Rhys blurted out.

"Rhys! Jeez. Liam and I are fine." Cameron shot straight back at his friend. The rest of the team was laughing now.

"Well, I'm glad to hear it, Cameron. It won't be a problem then if we end up playing them in the championships next weekend. Now, the rest of you settle down and pay attention to the rest of the tape," Coach John said, glaring at the boys. They all nodded. They knew better than to mess around when their coach had that look on his face.

They settled in and continued watching the game tape, with Tyler the trainer and Coach John pointing out some of the mistakes they'd made during the game. It wasn't often the teams were lucky enough to watch tapes like this and break down where they had gone wrong and what they had done right.

Millie and Georgia were at Millie's house hanging out after they had reviewed their game tapes.

"So, do you know what you're doing for your party this year, Mills?" Georgia asked sweetly.

"Of course. Well, I know I always do a skating party at the arena, but this year my parents asked if I wanted to do something different. My dad knows the guy that opened up that new trampoline park in town, so my dad said we could have a party for fifteen people and me."

"Wow, that's awesome. That place only just opened, but I heard from some of the other kids at school that it's pretty awesome."

"Yeah, my mom and dad showed me the website."

"So, who are you going to invite? Fifteen people, that's pretty much all the seniors from both hockey teams..."

"Yep. That's what I was thinking. My mom even said afterwards I could have a sleepover with all the girls who wanted to come over," Millie replied.

"Oh, that will be so cool. You have the best movie nights and sleepovers. Do you want a hand making the invitations? We can give them out at school tomorrow."

"Yeah, it's pretty late for invitations, but I think most people know I'm doing something anyway. We'll get them written out now; I think my mom has some cards downstairs."

Millie, Georgia, Mia, Lola, Khloe, Sage, Violet, Daylyn, and Ashlyn had all driven to Trampoline World with Millie's parents in two cars as they'd needed to drop their sleepover things off first. They wouldn't be going home afterward to get anything because they'd be going straight to Millie's after the birthday party at the trampoline place.

The girls were the first to arrive at the party because Millie's parents had food and decorations to set up in the party room. This meant they were the first ones to get the special trampoline socks.

"Well, we aren't going to get lost in these socks now, are we?" Khloe asked as she pranced up and down the lobby area as if she was a model on a catwalk in Paris. "I mean, they're pretty bright!"

This set all the girls to parading up and down, each trying to outdo the others with their dramatic walks.

"My little brother, Robbie, has these same socks," Lola said, rubbing the sole of her foot, "I mean they even have the same little plastic bumps on them."

While the girls all finished putting their socks on, the boys started to drift in and get their own special socks to put on. The older girl behind the counter explained to all the kids that the socks would give them extra traction on the trampolines. She then went on to explain the rules of Trampoline World and all the different areas the kids could play in.

They started off with a game of trampoline basketball that quickly turned into a noisy game of dodgeball. No one took either of the games very seriously, but by the time Millie's mom and dad

called them in for pizza and cake, they were all starting to get pretty worn out.

"Okay, everyone! I need five minutes of your time to cut the cake and sing Happy Birthday. After that, we'll do presents, and then you can all head back out onto the trampolines for another hour," Millie's mom announced, banging a knife against a glass to get all the kid's attention.

The kids all filed over to the table and started singing a little off-key but enthusiastically, "Happy birthday to you. Happy birthday to you. Happy birthday, dear Millie. Happy birthday to you!" They gave a loud round of applause at the end.

Millie tried her best to make herself as small as possible, but Mia and Cameron dragged her to the front of the room.

"Thanks, everyone. You guys are the best," she said quietly, her face bright red. Then she opened all the presents as fast as she could so they could all get back out to the trampolines before their time was up.

"Wow. My legs are so sore. I don't think I'm going to be able to walk properly tomorrow!" Khloe said from the mattress on the floor of Millie's large living room where all the girls were gathered.

"I thought goalies were supposed to be super flexible," Georgia piped up.

"We are! We're just not used to trampolining for hours at a time!" Khloe replied. "I'm built for flexing, not bouncing!" Khloe replied, throwing her pillow at Georgia, who caught it and hurled it straight back. Khloe dodged out of the way of the flying pillow, causing it to knock straight into Mia.

"Wow! What did I do?"

"Oops! Sorry, Mia. Wouldn't want to mess up that pretty face Cameron wants to smooch!" Georgia replied, giggling.

"Have you kissed Cameron?" Daylyn and Ashlyn, the twins, blurted out at exactly the same time.

"No!" Mia shouted back, blushing bright red.

"OMG! Do we always have to talk about boys? Gross!" Sage said, screwing her face up as if she had smelled something horrible.

"Sage is right. I mean, have you smelled their locker room? I swear half their gear could walk around by itself. It stinks so bad," Khloe added in.

"Cameron doesn't stink! I mean, well, after he's been wearing his hockey gear, he's a bit stinky, but—"

"So he does stink! See, they all stink," Violet interrupted, her point proven.

"Enough about boys. All we do is talk about boys and hockey!" Lola piped up.

"Sometimes we talk about lacrosse too," Khloe interrupted. "Just saying." This made all the girls start throwing pillows and whatever else they had handy at her. Khloe, never one to shy away from a fight, started hurling everything back. The pillow fight might have turned into all-out war if Millie's dad hadn't burst in to see what all the screaming was about.

They spent the rest of the night watching scary movies and eating popcorn late into the evening before they all eventually gave in and fell asleep.

When the girls woke up in the morning, they were greeted by the delicious aroma of pancakes and maple syrup drifting through the house. Millie's mom's pancakes were one of the best things about a sleepover at Millie's house. Her mom always had so many different toppings to choose from. Bananas, strawberries, chocolate chips, whipped cream, ice cream, and just about anything else you could imagine.

After everyone had eaten until they were about to burst, their parents started arriving to pick them up. This just left Millie to finish helping her mom clean up the bedding and mattresses and clean up after breakfast. *It really had been an awesome party*, Millie thought to herself as she finished drying dishes and putting them away.

"Thanks, Mom. I had heaps of fun," Millie said, giving her mom a hug when they'd finally finished cleaning everything.

"Well, what a nice surprise! You're welcome, Mills. Glad you had a great time."

Millie went upstairs to her room and threw herself down on the bed, grabbing her phone off the charger beside her bed. Liam had texted her while she'd been downstairs cleaning.

They texted back and forth about the upcoming championships and when they would be playing. All the teams played one game on Friday, two games Saturday, and then quarterfinals Saturday night if they made it through.

Millie played first on Friday, so she'd be able to watch both Cameron and Liam play their games afterward. Unfortunately, on Saturday, all three teams would be playing at roughly the same time, so it would be hard to watch each other's games.

Millie didn't realize just how tired she was from the sleepover, and before she knew it, she'd fallen asleep with her phone in her hand.

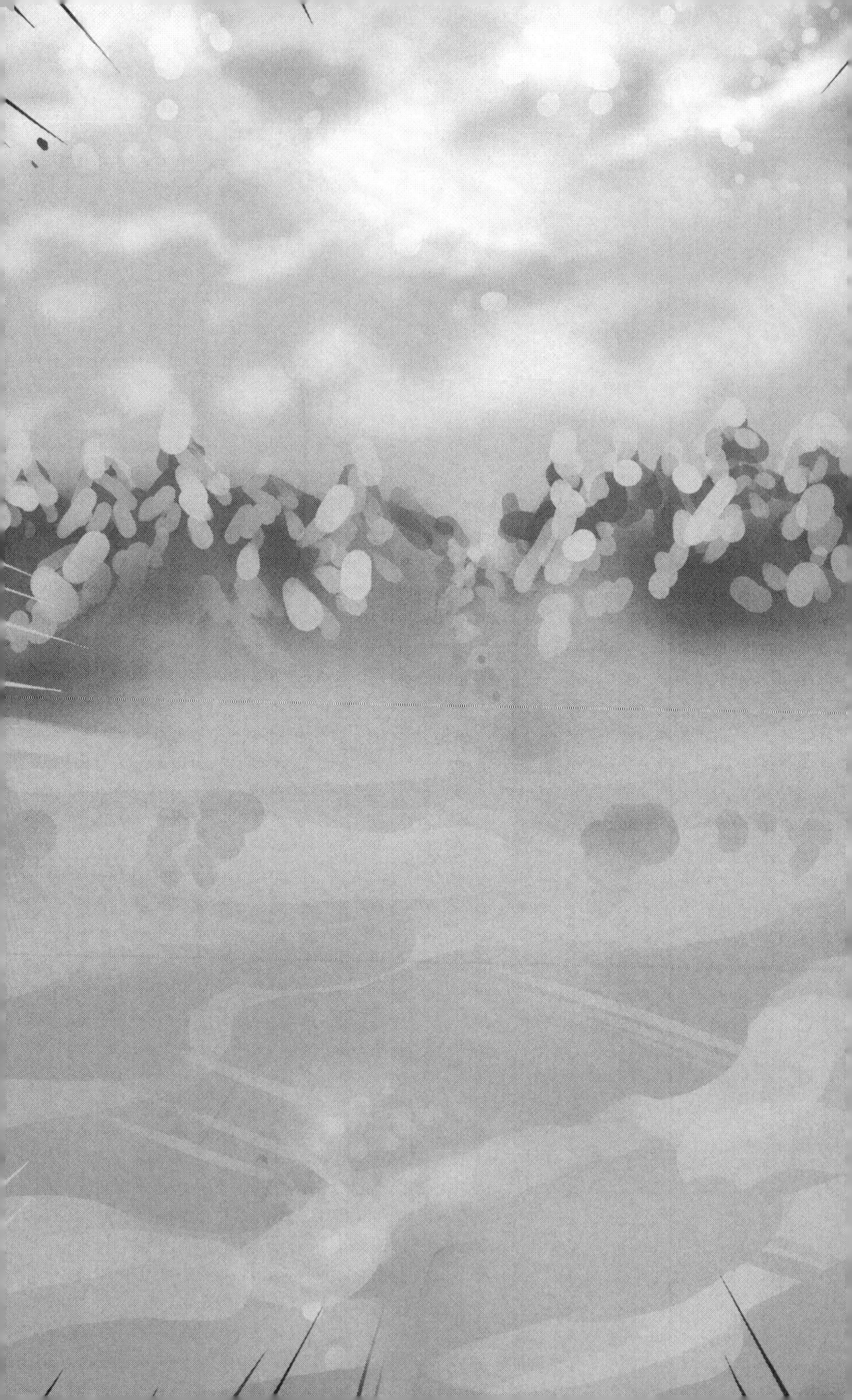

7

IT HAD BEEN a very intense week for the girls and boys of the Dakota Hurricanes and Lightning. Many of the kids had believed they'd get a rest before championships, but if anything, both coaches had stepped up their training routines. They had been focusing on stamina drills and speed, trying to fine tune the kids' skating skills before the championships.

"I didn't think it was possible to be this tired," Hunter said as they sat in the conference room at the arena watching different drill tapes.

"Dude. I hear you. Now, be quiet in case the coach hears us and makes us run laps. I'm too tired to move," Rhys replied, barely moving his head off the desk he was leaning on.

"It'll be worth it if we win championships," Linkin said.

"Linkin, I appreciate the sentiment, but you're not running around and around the arena with us." Rhys said quietly.

"Thanks for reminding me, Rhys. It's not like I wouldn't be out there if I could."

"He's right, Rhys, he didn't break his arm on purpose. So leave him alone." Cameron said shortly. Sometimes, well a lot of the time, Rhys opened his mouth without thinking about the words coming out and how they could hurt people.

"Look, sorry, Linkin. I didn't mean anything by it. I just hate running," Rhys said, apologizing and for once looking like he actually meant it. Linkin nodded and all three of the boys went back to watching the drill tapes their coach was playing.

The girl's week had been much the same, with two practice sessions on the ice and a night spent watching drill tapes in the conference room.

Despite all the kids' complaining, they were still pumped up about heading to the championships, with both teams heading into the weekend with a good chance of taking the title. For the small school, it was an exciting time as they hadn't had a championship team for many years.

If either of the teams was fortunate enough to win the championship, they would have bragging rights that would last longer than the remainder of the school year.

It was this very topic a few of the kids were talking about at lunch on Thursday, the last day of school before they left for the championships.

"Hockey is totally worth it just to get out of going to school tomorrow," Khloe said excitedly to the group of kids sitting around her eating their lunches in the cafeteria.

"It's cheeseburger and fries day tomorrow, though!" Rhys said quickly.

"True. Oh, that sucks. I hadn't thought about that part, but at least I'll miss out on the math quiz we were supposed to have," Khloe replied.

"They rescheduled it for Monday," Millie added.

"Are you serious?" Khloe and Rhys both chimed in.

"Afraid so," Mia added with a giggle.

"What is the point of getting out of class if we're not going to miss any of the sucky stuff? Not only that, but we're missing out on cheeseburger and fries day too!"

"Worst. Day. Ever!" Khloe added dramatically.

The rest of the kids couldn't help but laugh at Khloe and Rhys. Trust those two to be more disappointed about missing out on cheeseburgers than excited about the championships.

"On another note, I need a lift to championships. Both my mom and dad are working on the Friday and can't make it up until the afternoon. Has anyone got any space?" Mia asked. Once upon a time, this would have been a nerve-wracking conversation, but she had never felt more accepted in a group of friends than she had since arriving in Dakota. It had been a rough start with Millie, but they had soon become best friends.

"You can come up with me, Mia. Mom has plenty of room in her new SUV," Millie offered. It was almost a three-hour drive, and having someone to talk with would help pass some of the time.

"Aw, thanks Mills. I'll let my mom know I have a lift sorted out."

"No worries. If you like, you could stay over tonight. That'll save you from having to get up so early and getting your parents to drive you over."

"Are you sure that's going to be okay with your parents?" Mia asked.

"Yep. I always have someone staying over.

I don't think my mom would know what to do if there weren't a few extra kids hanging around the house," Millie replied with a laugh.

"Does anyone else need a lift?" Cameron asked. He would have liked to have given a Mia a lift up with him, but Millie had jumped in too fast for him.

None of the other kids needed a lift, and the conversation soon made its way back to hockey and how everyone's favorite NHL teams were doing. Each of the kids had their own favorite team, and there was always a lot of speculation about which team was going to make it into the playoffs and which wouldn't.

8

THE GIRLS' FIRST game was scheduled for 1:00 p.m., and they had to get to the arena a few hours before to get dressed and warmed up. This had led to them getting up early and hitting the road for the long three-hour drive.

Even though Mia had stayed over, both girls had gone to bed early so they'd be ready for the early-morning drive to championships and their first game. Millie's mom had packed a cooler of drinks and snacks for the road for the girls to eat along the way. They would eat enough junk over the weekend, and a few healthy snacks before the first game would help settle stomachs and nerves.

"Mom, turn this song up! We love this one!" Millie shouted at her mom.

The new pop song was doing the rounds of all

the radio stations at the moment, with a bunch of different celebrities doing their own version of the dance that went along with it. Millie's mom cranked up the volume in the SUV, and they all sang along, with the girls making their best attempts at dancing while strapped into their seat belts.

"I love that song!" Mia shouted at Millie.

"Me too. If we get a chance tonight, we should get all the girls together and do our own version. It would be awesome."

"Oh, that would be epic. We could do it wearing our jerseys or pajamas. It would be hilarious."

The rest of the long car trip went much the same way, with both girls—and even Millie's mom—joining in signing. If there was one way to make a three-hour car journey a little more fun, it was to get some of your friends to come with you.

Millie's mom and dad parked the SUV in the back parking lot, where all the other parents had agreed to meet. It meant they would be all be able to grab their kids when the games were done and head out in the same direction.

Despite them talking it down during the week, the girls were all getting very nervous about their first game. The state championships were for the best of the best after all, and winning here would go a long way toward cementing their place as one of the best teams in the country.

The girls didn't mess around, heading to the dressing room to start getting into their warmup gear. Their coach didn't yell as much as the boys' coach, but he could definitely raise his voice a few decibels when he was angry.

All the girls headed out to do their warmup exercises without any hassles. There wasn't a lot of talking as they all focused on the upcoming game and getting warmed up. No one wanted to get injured because they didn't take the time to stretch properly.

After their warmup, it was time to head back to their change room to finish putting on their equipment.

"I love away games and hanging out over the weekend, but wow, I hate driving for over three hours," Daylyn said, yawning, "I mean, that car ride was seriously long."

"It only felt long because you sulked and whined the whole away about how long it was," Ashlyn said to her sister. Daylyn didn't bother to reply, instead choosing to stick her tongue out at her sister.

"Okay, girls. That's enough of the chatter. I'll see you on the ice in ten minutes," Coach Phil said as he left the change room. The girls finished getting ready and then headed out onto the ice for the first time at the championships.

Millie skated out onto the ice and looked around the arena. The seats were full of hundreds of people. This was the most people she had ever played in front of before. This was crazy!

"You okay, Mills? You look like you're going to throw up?" Georgia asked as she skated over to where Millie was looking up into the crowded seats.

"Umm, yeah. There's a lot of people out there watching," Millie replied nervously.

"Look, don't worry about them. You're our captain, and we need our captain to be brave and confident, not throwing up all over the ice. You gotta pull yourself together." Georgia smiled nervously at Millie.

"You're right. Let's go over to the bench so Coach Phil can do his talk. It's almost time to start," Millie replied as the two senior players skated over to the bench to join the rest of the girls.

"Okay girls, this is game one of the championships. This is what we've all worked hard for all year. It's time to stop worrying about what could be and just play our best game. We're going to play this game our way. Don't worry about the crowds, and just focus on what we've been training for. Now, go get 'em, girls!"

The girls didn't mess around when the siren sounded at the start of the game. They took an early lead in the first period, finishing 2-0 after the siren sounded to halt play. Both teams skated to their benches and took a much-needed water break.

"Great effort, girls. You're all playing great. We're two up, but we need to keep our feet on the gas pedal and not give them a chance to get back into the game. Now, grab a drink and let's get back out on the ice!" Coach Phil clapped as the girls all cheered and headed out onto the ice for the second period.

It was another great period, with all the girls applying even more pressure. The team they were playing weren't ranked as high as them in the state, but all the teams playing were some of the best in the state. The girls put the puck into the net late in the second period to head into the third and final period, leading the game 3-0.

The last period of the game played out much

the same as the first two periods, with the other team failing to capitalize on several missed opportunities. Their defense was great, but their offense had missed a few close shots on goal because of Khloe's excellent goaltending.

When the final siren sounded signaling the end of the game, the girls were up 4-0. While the rest of the girls were celebrating, Millie skated up to the other goalie and made it a point to congratulate her on playing a great game. After all, it wasn't her fault her offense hadn't been able to help her out as much as they could have.

After the girls had changed, they checked on the boys. They still had a little while before they were scheduled to start their game, so most of the girls took the opportunity to wander around the different arenas.

There were so many different stands set up. Hockey equipment, jerseys, hockey cards, food stands, posters, temporary tattoos, temporary hair dye stations, and much more. The girls got to choose the Hurricanes' logo and get it put on their arms.

"These tattoos with our logo look so cool!" Khloe said as she flexed her arm.

"I know! I'm going to ask mom and dad if I can

get the rainbow hair dye later," Georgia said as she eyed all the different colors available.

"Me too! We should all get matching hair," Mia added.

"We'll try and set it up for later today or before tomorrow's game, but the boys are probably already on the ice, so we should start heading over," Mille said before they all got caught up and missed the boy's game.

9

THE BOYS' GAME had already started when the girls arrived. The Panthers, their opposing team, were supposed to be one of the best teams in the state, and it was going to be a tough start for the boys' championship run.

Even if you lost one of your early games, it didn't automatically rule you out of the championship, but it did make it harder later on. The goal was always to win all your games to give you the best draw when it came to playing in the finals. The lower teams always played the harder teams in the knockout stages later on.

The Panthers were playing a strong offensive game, which was keeping Logan on his toes. As soon as he'd stopped one shot, they would set up a play to have another go on the net.

"Dude! Come on. You have to get your stuff together and give me a chance here. I can keep blocking shots, but eventually, they're going to get lucky and find the back of the net," Logan shouted at Ben and Riley, his two defensive players. "Get your heads in the game!"

Riley put his head down and retrieved the puck, heading out of their defensive end toward the other end of the rink. With his focus on the players ahead of him, Riley didn't notice the opposition player coming in from his blindside.

The smaller boy slapped the puck off Riley's stick and skated back toward where Logan was covering their goal. Riley, furious with himself and off balance, slashed out at the other player and ended up accidentally connecting with him, tripping him.

The kid fell hard on the ice, with Riley tripping over him and sliding as he heard the referee blow the whistle.

"Tripping! Two-minute penalty."

"Come on! I told you he wasn't ready for this. He's going to cost us the game!" Rhys shouted angrily from the bench. Several of the other players were grumbling too. From where they sat, it looked like Riley had thrown a tantrum and taken the opposition player out on purpose.

"Rhys! Enough. It looked like an honest mistake. Now, cut out the chatter and focus on the game. Your line is up, and I need you to kill this penalty. Now, go get it done!" Coach John shouted.

Riley couldn't hear what was being said on the bench, but he heard the couch shouting and assumed it was about how he had messed up. He hung his head down and looked at his skates, trying his best not to start tearing up. *If they scored now, we could lose the game, and it's all my stupid fault*, Riley thought to himself, getting more and more upset as he watched his brother and the rest of the penalty kill team desperately defending against the opposing offense.

There were only seconds left on the penalty timer, and Riley was standing, ready to hit the ice. Just as the official reached for the door to let him out, the Panthers found a gap in Logan's defense, and the puck found its way into the back of the net.

"Jeez, that was so close. I thought they were going to make it," Mia said quietly from behind the glass where the girls were gathered watching the game.

"Wow, Riley looks devasted," Millie added. While Rhys' little brother could be an annoying little brat sometimes, they all knew what it felt like to be sitting in that penalty box when your team gets scored on. It felt like the loneliest little box on the planet.

The siren sounded to signal the end of the first period, and the score was 1-0 against the boys.

Coach John spent the break between the first and second periods trying to build the boys back up, but the damage had been done. They continued to struggle to find their feet during the next two periods, and despite a goal by Cameron late in the last period, the final score was 3-1 against the Lightning.

"It cost us the game! If they hadn't scored that first goal, we could..."

"Enough, Rhys! Cut it out. Now, I'm going to talk, and you're all going to listen with no interruptions. Riley, accidents happen. We all get nervous and make mistakes. You need to shake it off and get over it. There'll be time to make it up in another game. Everyone on this team has made mistakes, including me. It's how we use the lessons from those mistakes that defines us. It wasn't one big mistake that cost us the game, it was all the little mistakes. The biggest mistake we made was not playing as a team."

"You're right, Coach. We'll make it up to you," Cameron said, standing up.

"Don't make it up to me. Make it up to each other," Coach John answered him. "Now, we're having a team dinner tonight, and after that, we're going to be having a team meeting. Your parents already have all the details. Get changed and think about what I said and what really cost us the game today."

Riley was the first to finish getting changed out of his hockey equipment and rushed out of the change room with his head down. As he pushed his way past the line of parents and kids outside the change room, Millie could see he had tears on his face. *He really was taking this hard*, Millie thought to herself sadly.

Just then, Millie noticed Cameron come out of the room and pushed her way through the crowd of people gathered in the hallway to talk to him.

"Cameron, what's up with Riley? He looked like he'd been crying."

"Um, I don't know? The coach didn't yell at him at all. Just told us we didn't play as a team, and that cost us the game. Riley's usually the first one to make a joke, not let things bug him," Cameron replied.

"Well, I think he's taking that penalty much harder than you all realize. Maybe you should talk to him?" Millie said quietly.

"Okay. Once we get back to the hotel, I'll track him down and find out what's going on."

"Hey, Riley. Have you got a minute?" Cameron asked when he saw the younger boy slapping shots off his practice pad in the garden area behind the hotel. Riley looked up but didn't answer; instead, he just shrugged and continued slapping shots off the practice pad he'd put down in the grass.

"Come on, dude, you can't sulk about the game forever."

"I'm not sulking!" Riley said, taking a particularly savage shot.

"Come on, Riley. It's not your fault we lost the game. You were there. You heard what Coach John said after the game. We all lost that game, not just you or any one person."

"But I'm the one that cost us the first goal. I got the penalty. Now my brother hates me even more than usual. You don't understand. Rhys does everything perfectly, and I'm the one that messes things up," Riley said quietly.

Cameron couldn't help but burst out laughing.

"What's so funny?"

"Riley, your brother feels exactly the same way about you, and if you think Rhys is perfect, then you should ask the coach what he thinks when you get a chance. He spends more time yelling at Rhys than the rest of us combined. Don't worry about today. Put your hockey gear away and come and hang out with the rest of the team in the pool."

"Okay, Cameron. Thanks."

"Call me Cam. Everyone else does, and you're welcome. Anytime."

10

MILLIE WAS HANGING her hockey equipment in the hotel room bathroom, attempting to air it out before tomorrow's games, when she heard her phone buzz.

It was a text from Liam saying he'd won his first game and would be staying at the same hotel. Millie and Liam arranged to meet after dinner down by the hotel pool. Millie and Liam had previously met at a tournament and hit it off, despite them playing for different teams and coming from different towns. Liam and Millie had texted and called each other back and forth almost every day since. Eventually, Liam had asked Millie to be his girlfriend, and they had been dating, as much as was possible long distance, ever since.

Liam played for the Blue Devils, and his team

would probably end up playing against the boys' team sometime during the championships. Millie had been going to stay and watch his game, but her parents wanted to get checked into the hotel. There would be plenty of other opportunities for her to see him play over the weekend.

All the kids had sat down to a large spaghetti dinner, which the parents had organized. There were three different types of pasta to choose from as well as salads, garlic bread, and ice cream and cookies for dessert.

It was always good for team spirits and bonding to have the kids eat together. It also gave the parents the opportunity to hang out and get to know each other as well in a friendly and relaxed setting. Standing around the arena glass and screaming and cheering wasn't always the best way to get to know other people.

While the girls were celebrating their first win of the championships and were quite excited during dinner, the boys were still pretty quiet after their loss in game one, and most of them weren't looking forward to the team meeting after the dinner.

Coach John barely let the boys finish eating their dessert before loudly calling for them to meet him in the conference room.

"Okay, boys, I'm going to keep this very short. I know you're all excited to go and jump in the pool. Firstly, don't go crazy in the pool because you have a lot of hockey coming up. Secondly, forget about today's game. It's done and dusted. They didn't win that game; we lost it. It's plain and simple. No, Rhys, put your hand down. This is a me talking and you listening quietly kind of deal," Coach John said, cutting of Rhys before he could get his mouth half open. "Next time we play, we're going to play as a team and win or lose as a team. No member of this team is more or less valuable than another member of the team. So, not too much carrying on in the pool and get a good night's sleep. Think about the other guys on the team and how much you need each other. Now, goodnight. The curfew is 8:30 p.m., in your rooms." With that, Coach John stood and ushered the boys out of the conference room.

"Seriously, that was a short meeting dude," Rhys said to Cameron as they headed toward the elevators. All the kids needed to go and get towels and swimwear so they could hit the pool before their curfew.

"I know, but at least he didn't scream at us this time," Cameron replied, relieved. "But you know, you could give Riley a break maybe. I know it sucks having your little brother on the team, but he is your brother, and he's pretty upset about the game. Besides, we've all made mistakes in games before."

"He cost us the game, though."

"Hey, no one's perfect. What about that time you got sent off in the last two minutes, and the other team scored during the power play, and it cost us the game?" Cameron reminded Rhys as the elevator doors quietly hissed shut.

"Yeah, but I was..." Rhys started to mumble before Cameron continued.

"You were what, new? Well, guess what? So is Riley. He's also your little brother, and he's feeling pretty terrible. So, how about acting like a big brother and helping him instead of bugging him all the time?"

"Huh. Guess I hadn't seen it like that." Rhys said quietly.

"So, why don't you grab Riley and meet us all down at the pool?"

"All right. I'll go grab him and get changed and meet you down by the pool," Rhys said to Cameron as the elevator doors opened on their floor. "Hey, thanks for that."

"Anytime. Whenever your head gets too big for your body, you can count on me to pop it," Cameron said, laughing and punching his friend on the arm as the two headed off to their rooms to get changed.

"Hey, Cameron, you heading down to the pool?" Liam asked when he saw Millie's best friend, Cameron, leaving his hotel room with his towel.

"Um, yeah, we're all going down. We have an 8:30 curfew, so we need to get in before the coaches change their minds," Cameron replied.

"Cool. Well, I guess if I don't see you later, I'll see you out on the ice at some point."

"Hey, why don't you come down to the pool too? We both know Millie isn't going to mind," Cameron said, laughing.

"I'd love to, but I have two of my teammates staying with me, Greyson and Luke."

"Bring them too. Isn't Georgia dating Greyson anyway?" Cameron replied. This conversation was quite a change since they'd first met on the

705
HOCKEY

ice at the last tournament. Cameron and Liam had almost come to blows on the ice before they'd finally settled things.

"Well, I guess yeah, that would be cool. I'll grab them and get changed. Just give me a minute," Liam said, ducking into his room quickly.

It seemed only a minute had gone by before Liam, Greyson, and their teammate, Luke, emerged back out into the hallway in their board shorts.

"We're ready! Let's go. Luke just told me our curfew is 8:30 too, so let's make the most of it before we all get sent off to our rooms," Liam replied as the four boys made their way toward the elevator.

On the ride down in the elevator, the four boys introduced themselves and talked about what position they played. When the four boys walked into the pool area together, Millie, Georgia, and some of the other girls were speechless. None of them expected them, opposing boys, to be hanging out together after their last meeting on the ice.

"Hey, Millie, Georgia, Mia, I'd like to introduce you to Liam, Greyson, and Luke. They're..."

"We know who they are silly," Mia replied, cutting her boyfriend off midsentence.

"Oh yeah, I guess you do!" Cameron said, winking at Millie and Georgia, who just rolled their eyes. "Anyway, we only have an hour, so, like we said earlier, we're going to play volleyball in the pool if any of you girls would like to join us?"

"We're actually just going to watch. Khloe is the only one that wanted in, so she'll probably play with you guys," Millie replied. Georgia, Mia, and the other girls nodded in agreement.

"All right, then. You're missing out. Cannonball!" Cameron screamed as he ran and jumped into the pool. Rhys and Riley had just walked into the pool area, and seeing Cameron jump in, they didn't waste any time dropping their towels and doing a synchronized leap into the pool just beside Khloe, completely covering her with pool water.

"Dudes! Seriously!" Khloe said, grabbing Riley and Rhys and dunking them both as soon as their heads popped up.

The rest of their time in the pool was spent with the boys playing volleyball and the girls chatting and splashing, and lots of laughter and screaming. Several times, Coach Phil and Coach John popped their heads into the pool room and told them to keep the noise down.

It wasn't long before their time was up, and all

the kids had to get out of the pool and head up to their rooms for curfew. Liam and Millie found themselves walking together to the elevator.

They managed to slip into the elevator and close the door before anyone else had a chance to jump in.

"That was fun! It was nice of Cameron to ask us to come down," Liam said.

"Yeah, I'm glad you two are getting along. He really is a good friend. He's like my brother, always looking out for me," Millie replied.

"I can see that. Anyway, it was good to hang out with you too. We don't get a lot of time together," Liam said quietly before reaching his hand out toward Millie's hand. Millie's heart almost stopped beating, and she could feel her face turning bright red as she moved her hand toward Liam's, closing the distance before their fingers touched.

When Millie finally looked up, she noticed Liam's face was bright red too. This made both of them giggle uncontrollably, and they were still laughing as the elevator doors slid open on their floor.

"I'm up this way," Millie said, pointing up the hallway.

"I'm up the other end. I'll text you?" Liam replied, finally letting Millie's hand go.

"That would be nice. See you tomorrow!" Millie said as she waved goodbye and started walking toward her room. As she got to the bend in the hallway, Millie looked back over her shoulder and locked eyes with Liam, who was doing exactly the same thing! The two them both started laughing again, then waved a final goodbye.

11

BOTH TEAMS HAD a big day ahead of them, with two games to play and then a quarter-final game if they made it that far. The boys had a little bit more work to do to make up for their loss on Friday if they were to stand any chance of making it into the finals.

Most of the kids, parents, and coaches were in the hotel lobby taking advantage of the buffet breakfast when Millie made her way down from her room.

"Mills! We saved you a spot!" Georgia shouted from a large table by the window.

"Yeah, but we didn't save you any bacon!" Khloe shouted, rubbing her stomach dramatically, "We ate all the baconnnn!"

Millie didn't respond. Instead, she just rolled

her eyes dramatically before heading toward the food. Just like the girls had said, there was no bacon. She didn't usually like to eat fatty foods, but before a big day like today, it was important to load up on food that would fuel her body.

Lucky for her, there were still plenty of sausages left. As a bonus, they also had waffles and pancakes and a whole bar full of fresh fruit, yogurt, and cereal.

"Morning, Mills," Liam said, lining up behind her. It was no coincidence they'd both showed up late for breakfast. They had been upstairs texting each other since they woke up.

"Hey, Liam," Millie replied, smiling and blushing as she saw several of her teammates laughing and whispering while watching her and Liam.

"You want to sit and eat breakfast?"

"I would, but the girls have already saved me a spot, and I don't have long to eat. I already dropped my bag near the front door, so I can just eat and head out. Maybe tomorrow?" Millie replied.

"That's cool, and for sure. Anyway, good luck with your games today, and I'll try and watch as much as I can. See you!" Liam said, grabbing his plate and getting ready to head over to where his team was gathered.

"Thanks, Liam. Good luck to you as well and ditto!"

The girls were playing first, followed by the boys.

The girls were playing the Stars, who were well known to have a massive defensive line. As the girls warmed up out on the ice, they couldn't help but wonder how they were going to get through that human wall of players.

"Seriously, what are they feeding those defense girls?" Mia asked as she slid to a stop next to the bench, where Millie and Georgia were stretching. "They're huge!"

"The bigger they are, the harder they fall!" one of the junior girls said as she skated past, getting a laugh from some of the other girls on the ice.

The girls were five minutes into the first period, and the scores were tied at 0-0. Neither team had managed to score, even though the Hurricanes had been given two power plays after the other team had been penalized for some overzealous defensive work.

Millie was breathing hard as she hit the bench after their last power play had failed to get them on the board.

"Their defense is so good, and their penalty kill line is amazing!" she said to the coach between taking mouthfuls of water from her sports bottle.

"I know, but we're better overall, and their offense is no match for us. We need to capitalize on the next penalty, and there will be another one. Those defense players are too rough, and the refs are watching them like hawks," Coach Phil replied.

"So, what's the plan?" one of the junior players, Averie, asked quietly.

"We stick to the game plan. We play our game, not theirs. The next time we have a power play, I want Millie, Georgia, and Mia on the ice. Between the three of you, I know you'll get the puck in the net."

They didn't have to wait long to see if Coach Phil's plan would work. The Stars defense took Kiera, one of the Hurricanes' juniors, down hard in the Stars' zone, and the referees called a two-minute penalty.

Mia, Millie, and Georgia didn't mess around and hit the ice fast, heading to their end for the face off. Millie lost the draw and the puck went sailing down the ice. No icing was called as they had a penalty. The three girls grabbed the puck and pushed hard up the ice. The Stars' best penalty kill line hadn't expected the speed of the three girls coming back up the ice.

Millie blew through the first two defense players, then faked to her left, leaving the puck behind her. Georgia, who was right on her heels, wound up and smashed the puck into the top right corner of the net.

The goal had ended the penalty, but it gave the girls a chance to grab some water on the bench while the referees set up again.

"Good work, girls. Next time, the same thing. If they're going to play rough, then we're going to punish them on the scoreboard all day long!" Coach Phil said loudly enough for the whole bench to hear.

The girl's joy was short-lived, however, as only a few minutes later, the Stars evened the score with a powerful push forward.

Millie was skating up the ice with Mia by her side, heading for the Stars' net, when she was blindsided, her legs taken out from under her. She slid along the ice and smashed into the boards hard.

Millie was slow trying to get up, and their trainer came out onto the ice with Coach Phil to make sure she was okay before helping her back

to the bench. The rest of the players on the ice had taken a knee while they waited to make sure she was okay.

"Are you feeling sick or dizzy, Millie?" their trainer asked as she sat on the bench, sipping from her water bottle.

"No, I'm okay. That was just a brutal landing. I think my butt might be bruised for a week!" Millie replied, attempting to rub her thigh through her pants.

"Okay. Well, there are only a few minutes left in this period, so you can sit out the next few shifts and go back out when the next period starts."

The siren finally sounded, signaling the end of the first period. The score was 1-1. It was going to be a long, hard game.

It was late in the second period, and neither team had managed to put another score on the board, despite some great plays. Both goalies had an amazing second period, with nothing getting by them.

Millie and Georgia found themselves skating up the ice again in much the same position they had earlier in the first period when Millie had been smashed into the boards. *Hopefully this time, it won't end up the same way*, Millie thought to herself.

This time Millie saw the defense player coming and quickly passed the puck over to Georgia. The defense player changed direction, attempting to intercept the puck before Georgia could get to it, but Georgia was quicker.

She recovered the puck and sent it back to Millie, who was closing in on the goal. Millie faked left and then sent the puck flying through the goalie's five-hole.

The Hurricanes were up 2-1 as the siren sounded to signal the end of the second period.

The third period started off much like the first two periods: rough.

Kiera was skating along the boards when she was taken out hard again, landing awkwardly and forcing the trainer and Coach Phil back onto the ice for the second time that game.

"Hey, Ref!" Coach Phil called out as the opposition player was being led to the penalty box. It was the Stars' seventh penalty of the game. "This is supposed to be noncontact. How about calling the hits before someone gets seriously hurt?" The referee didn't answer the coach's question, but he did remind him of the rules regarding coaches speaking to referees.

The referees started calling the opposition a little more consistently for the rest of the third period, but it didn't help. It was still an extremely rough last period, with the Stars desperately trying to score.

But they never managed to get through the Hurricanes' defense, with Khloe on fire in the last period and stopping several shots that would almost certainly have gone through with a less experienced goalie.

The girls rushed off the ice after the final siren sounded, hitting the change rooms to drop their hockey gear off. If they hurried, they'd be able to make it to the last thirty minutes of the boy's game.

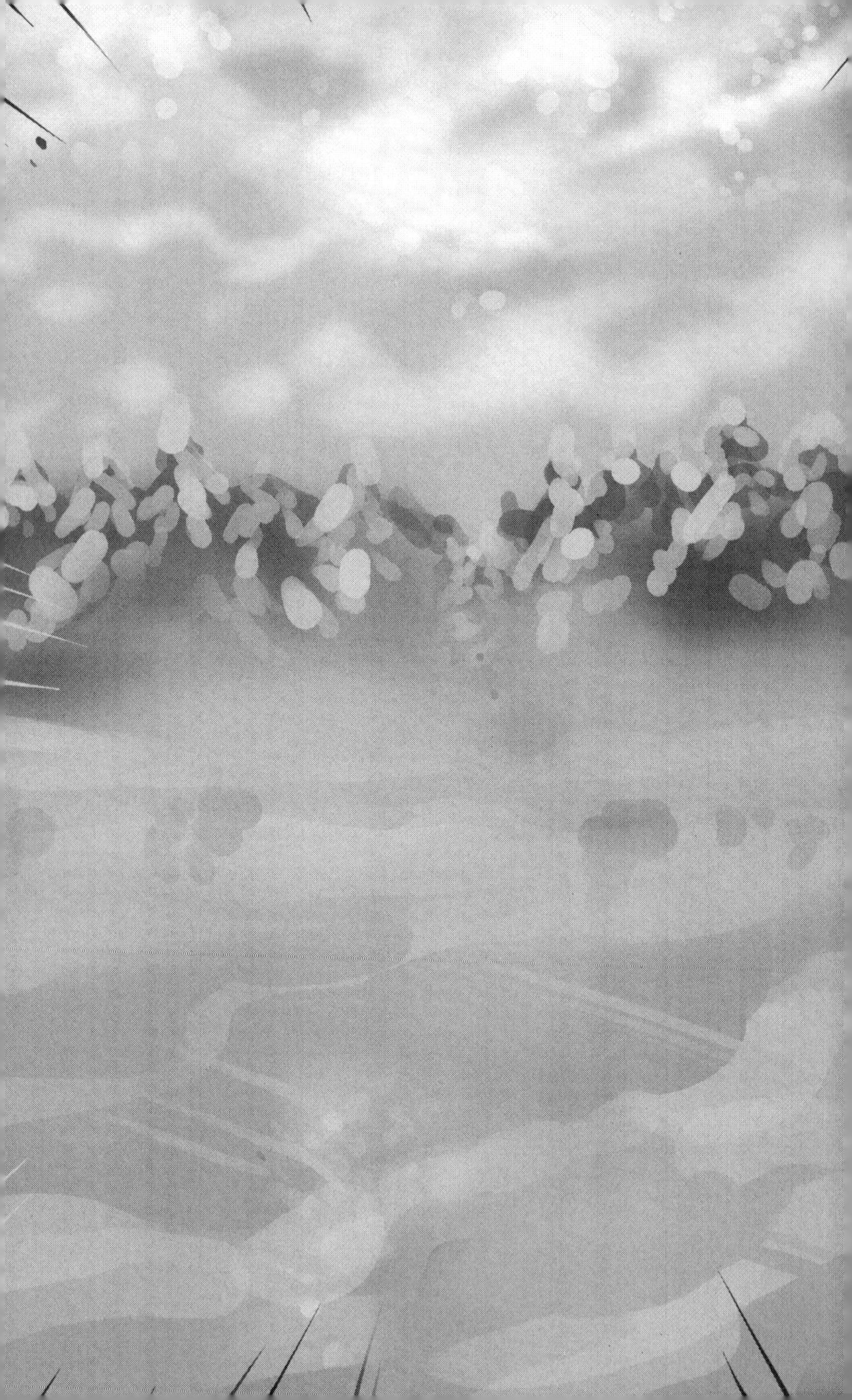

12

THE GIRLS PUSHED their way through the crowd of people toward the glass surrounding the arena the boys were playing on, just making it to the glass as the siren sounded, signaling the end of the first period. The game was slightly behind, the girls hadn't missed as much as they thought they would have.

"Wow, they're up two goals to nothing! That should put all of them in a good mood; they weren't much fun moping around like they were last night," Georgia said to the group of girls.

Khloe came up behind them, pushing and shoving her way through to where all the girls were standing. It was quite impressive she'd managed to get there right behind the other girls considering how much more gear she had to get off compared to the rest of them.

"Looks like Coach John won't be walking around giving us all the stink eye again tonight. As long as the boys don't blow it, that is," Khloe said with a laugh.

"Jeez, Khloe, don't jinx them. Sheesh," Mia said, shaking her head and laughing. Khloe hadn't been born with a filter. Whatever random thought popped into her head came straight out of her mouth a few seconds later, regardless of what it was, what she was thinking, or where she was.

The boys had come out of their change room at the beginning of this game with a new attitude after their defeat in the previous game. Coach John was impressed with the first period of the game, with the Lightning up 2-0 over the other team.

"Great work, guys. Cameron, Rhys, Riley, Hunter, and Reid, great pressure. Now, we have them 2-0, and I expect you guys to keep applying pressure. We lost the first game yesterday, so it's important we finish this game as strongly as possible. Now, get back out there, and let's put some more scores on the board!"

The boys cheered and headed out to their positions on the ice. The boys from the Hornets took their time coming out of their huddle. Obviously, their coach was trying to inspire his kids to pick up the pace and make up the score.

"Ready to go again, Riley? We'll try and get you a goal," Cameron asked as they waited with the referee, who was waiting for the other team's centerman so he could drop the puck for the faceoff.

"Yep, hopefully. It would help make up for yesterday for sure," Riley answered. When Riley had come out on the ice, both he and his big brother had been like two new kids. They hadn't fought or argued once. What Cameron noticed most of all was that when they were both on the ice on the same shift, they could predict what the other was going to do. If they could keep that up, Riley and Rhys would make an awesome addition to their team.

Millie had been hoping she'd be able to watch some of Liam's game, but he was playing at the same time on the other side of the complex. She could have walked back and forth, but she would miss parts of both games. Instead, she'd decided to watch Cameron and the boys play this game, then go and watch Liam's game with Georgia next time.

The Hornets came out strong in the second period, trying to take advantage of their size to outmuscle the Lightning boys on the ice. At first, the Lightning had to take a step back and regroup, but they didn't buckle under the pressure.

"Man, what did they drink during that break?" Rhys said as he slid onto the bench after his shift on the ice. The other team hadn't managed to press their advantage so far, but there had been a few close calls, and only some exciting and athletic goalkeeping by Logan had kept them from scoring.

"I don't know, but I wish we had some," Luke laughed. Luke was one of Cameron's close friends. He'd been pretty aggressive out on the ice the entire game, but the pressure so far in the second period had just about worn him out.

"Me too," Rhys replied, looking up at the scoreboard to see how many minutes were left in the second period. *Five minutes*, he thought to himself. May as well be five hours the way his legs felt at the moment.

Coach John looked down at the two boys talking and noticed that not only was Rhys quieter than usual, he was staring up at the scoreboard. It was a sure sign things were either not going well, or the boys were starting to get tired.

"Five minutes left to go in this period, boys. I want you to take it easy on the next shift unless an opportunity presents itself. We'll try and rush something through in the last few minutes," Coach John said to the boys on the bench.

Cameron slid through the open bench gate and slumped down onto his seat. Panting for breath, he too looked up at the clock.

"I was just telling some of the others to try and get a rest on this shift, and we'll push them for the last minute. I know you're tired, but look at their bench. They're even worse, and they're two goals down," Coach John said to Cameron.

It wasn't unusual for the coach to share his ideas with Cameron. As captain, it was Cameron's responsibility to motivate and encourage the rest of the guys on the team.

"No worries, Coach. Do you have a play in mind?"

"I think we'll go with the wheel on the breakout. Their forwards are gassed already. The wheel around the net should give you enough of a head start to set up your wingers. After that, you either take the shot or drop the puck to Rhys," Coach John said as he drew the play on his miniature whiteboard. Not all the players were as advanced on the plays as the seniors, so he found it helped to illustrate his point by sketching out the plays.

The next shift out on the ice, Cameron was

ready when he chased the loose puck down into their end. Logan came out of his net and bumped the puck toward Cameron with his goalie stick. It was a risky move, with the player hot on Cameron's heels. If Cameron missed it, Logan would have to scramble to get back into his net, but he knew Cameron wouldn't miss it.

Cameron swooped the puck up easily and wheeled around behind their net, and as they'd thought, the player chasing Cameron was already several lengths behind and failing to keep up.

Cam passed the puck up to his right side, where Riley grabbed the puck, skated hard over the blue line, and sent the puck around the boards, behind the opposition net to where Rhys was skating hard to get it. Rhys beat his man and quickly looked up to see Riley and Cam trying to break free from the defense. He saw a chance and passed it to Cam.

Time was ticking down fast; there were only thirty seconds left on the clock in the second period.

Cam picked up the puck cleanly as he tried to break free from the defense, but one defenseman was all over him, so he circled to the outside and flicked the puck back around to Rhys, who came low to support him on the other side of the net.

Rhys didn't miss a beat, but either did the defenseman. He was ready, and they hadn't left Rhys alone to go after Cam at all as he had hoped. Rhys decided to pass it over to his brother, who he saw circling in front.

The defense was getting tired and scrambling to keep up with the Lightning forwards, who just kept moving. They didn't react in time to Rhys's pass to Riley though. Riley circled, got open, and took a one-timer at the net.

The goalie slid desperately to his right side, expecting the shot to go fast and low, but it never happened and went top corner instead.

Goal! Only seconds later, the siren sounded, signaling the end of the second period.

Cam, Rhys, and Riley skated together toward the bench where the rest of the team was on their feet, cheering.

"Bro! Nice goal!" Rhys shouted, fist-bumping his little brother.

"He's right. That was an awesome shot. Congrats on your first goal in this division," Cameron said, slapping Riley on the back.

"Great job, boys, and nice shot, Riley. Now, enough chit chat. We only have a few minutes to rest and get a drink before the last period

starts," Coach John said. Rhys waited until Coach John wasn't looking and made a grumpy face, then winked at Cameron. "That includes pulling faces, Rhys. Don't think I won't have you doing sprints tonight."

The boys all put their hands over their mouths to stifle the laughter. They all knew Coach John wouldn't hesitate to follow through with his threats.

The last period was a grueling back and forth match between the two teams. The Hornets were exhausted, so they were playing a strong defensive game. They just didn't have the energy to push hard on both offense and defense.

The Lightning wasn't in much better shape. They were three goals up and had another important game coming up in three hours. Coach John told the boys to keep applying pressure, but they also had to play a defensive game.

As the minutes counted slowly down, it was like two heavyweight boxers at the end of the last round. They were both still standing, but neither were landing any blows.

As the siren sounded, signaling the end of the

game, the boys cheered and clapped along with the audience. The Lightning had won their second game of the championships 3-0.

The win was much more important than that, though, for this group of boys. They had played this game as a team and won.

13

BY THE TIME the boys finished getting their equipment off after their first game of the day, there were only three hours left until they had to be back on the ice. Usually, they would head back to the hotel or go out somewhere for lunch, but a particularly nasty snowstorm had settled in over the town where the championships were being held.

Instead, several of the parents had headed out into the storm to grab some lunch supplies from the grocery store close by. It would be an impromptu arena picnic for lunch today.

The kids from both the Lightning and Hurricanes made their way up to a quiet spot in the bleachers overlooking one of the arenas to eat their lunch and watch one of the older teams play.

Several of the parents arrived carrying large trays of sandwiches. There was a mad scramble by all the kids to try and get their favorites. If you weren't quick enough, you wouldn't miss out, but you might just end up eating something boring.

"What did you get?" Cameron asked Mia as they sat down together to eat their lunch.

"Ham and cheese. My least favorite. I wasn't quick enough," Mia huffed, looking suspiciously at her ham and cheese like it had something gross in it.

"Oh. I love ham and cheese. I'll swap you a turkey and swiss?" Cameron replied.

"Sweet. Deal." While Cameron and Mia swapped sandwiches and chatted about some of the highlights of their games, Liam, Greyson, and some of their teammates from the Blue Devils arrived with their own lunches.

Most of the talk centered around hockey. You would have thought they could find something else to talk about, but for these kids, hockey was their life. They wouldn't have it any other way.

All the coaches had given the kids strict orders to relax. No ball hockey and no running around the arena for the next few hours. All the teams had another game in a few hours, and depending on what happened, possibly a quarter-final game

later in the day. They would need to conserve all their energy for hockey.

"You guys want to come and check out some of the swag stands?" Rhys asked as he and Riley made their way down toward where Cameron, Mia, and the others were sitting. "My parents gave us some money to pick out some stuff. Coming?"

"Nah, I think I'm just going to hang out here," Cameron replied. Hunter, Khloe, and several of the other kids, though, went to check out the swag stores with the brothers while the rest just watched the game and chatted.

It seemed like they had been hanging out and chatting for only minutes when Millie looked up at the giant scoreboard and noticed it was already 11:00 a.m. *Time flies when you're having fun*, she thought to herself.

"Um, we have to go to girls. We have a game in an hour. The coach will tear strips off us if we're late," Millie said as she stood and grabbed her equipment bag.

"Wow. That went fast. Okay, I'll walk down through the swag area and grab Khloe and the others if they're still down there. Meet you at the change room. See you later, Cam, and good luck," Mia said as she stood up and brushed the crumbs off herself.

"Yeah, you too. We're playing thirty minutes after you, so we won't be able to watch. Sorry," Cameron said with disappointment. It was fun to watch each other's games, but it wasn't unusual for them to have overlapping schedules.

"It's okay, Cam; it's not your fault. See you later!" Mia said as she and the other girls made their way down the steps toward the exit.

Cameron, Liam, Greyson, and some of the other boys that were left decided to go and watch one of the teams from their division play on the rink next door. It would be an excellent opportunity for them to check out one of the teams they may end up having to play tonight or tomorrow.

All the boys were standing at the glass, watching the Trenell Golden Hawks play the Argyle Avengers.

"Dude. The Avengers are getting smashed out there. I thought they were ranked almost at the top of the division?" Logan asked.

"They're above us, and we're above you. But the Golden Hawks are the best team in the division if you look at their stats," Greyson said. No one ever liked to admit when another team was better than them, but the boys were all starting to get a little more worried about their championship hopes.

"All right, guys, we have to go warm up. We'll catch you all later after our game. What time are you playing?" Cameron asked Liam and the other Blue Devils.

"We're on the ice at 1:30. Good luck with your game, Cam," Liam replied.

"Okay, cool. Well, good luck to you too, and we'll swing by after our game and watch the end of yours," Cameron said as he and the rest of the Lightning started to head off to their change room.

"No worries. See you later, guys!"

14

THE GIRLS OF the Dakota Hurricanes came out strong for their second game of the day and their last scheduled game of the championships. They took the win 4-1 over the Bandits, who had been coming off a hard loss earlier in the morning.

The girls were now guaranteed a spot in the quarter-finals.

Millie had started them off strongly, scoring two goals within the first five minutes of the first period. The rest of the first period had been relatively quiet, with the Bandits going on the defensive while they tried to work out the Hurricanes' playing style.

The second period had seen the Hurricanes come out strongly again, with Georgia taking them to an impressive 3-0 lead. The Bandits had wasted no time, though, quickly following up with a slap shot on goal, which had snuck through Khloe's pads.

It was the Hurricanes' turn to switch to the defensive then, killing time until the clock signaled the end of the second period.

Coach Phil had used the break between periods to help the girls refocus on the game and had reminded them it was their offensive style of play that had put them in such a good position. Changing their playing style to match the Bandits could end up losing them the game, despite their impressive lead.

He needn't have worried.

Mia had come out strong and blown straight through the Bandits' defense within the first five minutes of the third period beginning. She'd taken the puck all the way to the net and scored an impressive goal on an already struggling goalie. It had shattered whatever hopes the Bandits had had left.

The rest of the game had been spent with the Bandits stacking their defense; the Hurricanes had been unable to penetrate and score again. They'd finished strong with a 4-1 win, crushing the Bandits' championship run.

The girls didn't mess around once they got off the ice. If they hurried, they would be able to watch the end of the boy's game before Liam and the Blue Devils played at 1:30.

The boys weren't as excited as they had been before seeing the Golden Hawks demolishing their opposition, but they were still pumped to try and win their third game.

The first period of the game saw both teams sitting on a 0-0 score. It wasn't for lack of trying, with both the Lightning and Brandon Bears putting down some amazing plays out on the ice, but they just couldn't find the net with both goalies on fire! The Lightning defense was struggling in the first period, but Logan kept the puck out of the net when it mattered most.

When the siren sounded, signaling the end of the first period, the boys were starting to get a little concerned, but Coach John was having none of it.

"Where is the team that showed up this morning ready to play?!" he shouted. "What happened to those kids? I can see a few of you hanging your heads. It's not the time or place for quitting. I won't

16
66

have it. You're starting to act like we've already lost when we've only just started. Now, defense, I want you in position and covering your man. Offense outmuscle them. They're good skaters, so show them who controls this ice. Okay?"

"Yes, Coach!" the boys shouted back.

"I didn't hear you!" Coach John shouted back even louder than before.

"Yes, Coach!" they chorused together loudly as a team.

"That's better! And Logan, keep up the good work. Now, get out there and show them who owns this ice!"

The boys hit the ice in the second period with renewed vigor. It appeared Coach John's speech had gotten through to them.

They stacked on three goals in the second period and it was looking like they would win the game easily. With the girls cheering them on from the side, they were heading into the last period in an excellent position to take the win.

Cameron and Riley had both scored one goal each and Hunter had gotten a lucky deflection off the goalie's pads to score his first goal of the game.

When the boys started the third period, it was

the Bears' turn to come out swinging! They hit the ice hard, and within sixty seconds, had put their first score of the game on the board. Before the Lightning even had a chance to regroup, the Bears were on the move again.

They pulled their goalie in a desperate attempt to outmuscle the Lightning with an extra player. The ploy worked. In a big push up the ice, they managed to open up the Lightning defense—and despite a desperate attempt by Logan—they managed to score.

The rest of the game turned into a back and forth, with the Lightning switching to a strong defensive lineup and the Bears going all in on their offense. There were only minutes left in the last period, and the Hurricanes were holding the other team off.

With sixty seconds on the clock, the Bears pulled their goalie and went six on five, but it was no use. The final siren sounded, and the score was 3-2, with the Hurricanes taking their second win.

Some of the girls, including Millie and Georgia, headed over to watch the Blue Devils game. Liam and his team had just started, so they would only have missed a few minutes if they didn't take too long to get there.

The girls found Liam's game just as the Blue Devils' goalie made an epic save.

"Wow. I can't believe how good that goalie is. He's more flexible than me!" Khloe said loudly.

Millie and Georgia just laughed. *There really was no filter on that girl*, Millie thought to herself.

"Liam told me his name is Finn. Apparently, he's going to play for the Highland Academy team next year," Georgia told Khloe.

"Do you think we'll be stuck here all afternoon?" Millie asked the group.

"My parents said it's almost white-out conditions out there," Isabelle, one of the juniors said. "The hotel is only like fifteen minutes away, but none of the parents want to risk getting stuck at the hotel and not being able to get back to the arena in time for the next game."

"Aw, man. That sucks," Georgia said, pouting.

The girls all got comfortable in the stands. No one was in any hurry to go anywhere as it looked as if they would be stuck there for several hours, and they weren't scheduled to play until 5:00 p.m.

The Blue Devils won their game 3-0. As games

went, it had been pretty boring, with the Blue Devils never looking as if they'd lose. Millie and the other girls started a mini Blue Devils cheer squad in the stands. Several of the little children came and sat with them, joining in the cheering whenever there was an exciting play.

The Hurricanes had several hours to wait until their next game, and with no running around allowed, it could be a long wait at the arena.

15

THE HURRICANES, BLUE Devils, and Lighting were heading to the quarter-finals, with the Hurricanes and Blue Devils undefeated and the Lighting sitting at 2-1.

Due to the blizzard conditions outside, the arena had opened its large meeting rooms for teams to set up small areas where the kids could eat and relax. Most teams had elected to stay, which meant no games were canceled, but they were already running thirty minutes behind on almost every game.

The girls were getting restless in their change room. Not only were they stuck at the arena all day, now they had to deal with the game being thirty or forty minutes late starting.

Coach Phil was doing his best to keep them

occupied, running them through a long list of stretches and warm-up exercises in the change room. Despite this, there was only so long you could keep kids occupied, and the delay was beginning to influence morale.

While they had been waiting for the game to start, Coach Phil had been filling the girls in on their opposition, the Perth Panthers. The girls knew they must be decent, otherwise, they wouldn't have made it this far.

Coach Phil explained that the Panthers had two good girls on their team, but they were greedy. They scored a lot of the Panthers' goals but didn't like to share the puck. For every game those two helped the Panthers win, there was another game where their greediness cost them the win.

The girls finally heard the siren sound, signaling the end of the previous game. This caused a rush for the door of the change room so they could get out on the ice and not waste any of the little warmup time they'd get before their game.

The quarter-final started great, with the girls settling in and getting a goal halfway through the first period. But their joy was short lived.

One of the twins, Daylyn, was called on a body contact penalty that put the girls down one player for two minutes. With only one minute left in the first period, Coach Phil put Millie, Mia, Ashlyn, and Emma out on the ice to defend. They were his best penalty kill line, and he needed them to be on fire.

The last minute of any period was when they were most often scored on. The girls all got a little distracted then, and that's when they made mistakes.

Fortunately, the girls managed to ice the puck twice and end the period with the score still 1-0. They still had another minute left on the penalty going into the second period, but things were looking good.

"You ready to do it again?" Millie asked the three other girls as they took the ice after the break between the first and second periods. They all nodded, looks of determination etched on their faces.

The last minute of the penalty ended up being anticlimactic, with the four girls spending the entire minute in the Panthers' end.

Daylyn burst out of the penalty box, determined to make up for her mistake, but thankfully the Panthers hadn't been able to take advantage of their opportunity and put a score on the board.

On a faceoff in the Panthers' end, Mia won the puck, sending it back to Daylyn. The rest of the forwards rushed the net as Daylyn wound up to take the shot. She sent the puck flying with an impressive slap shot. She'd always been proud to be one of the only girls on the team with such a strong slap shot.

It was a clean shot, with the puck flying off her stick in a blur. The Panther goalie struggled to see the shot as the players were all sticking firm, crowding the front of the net. The Panther defense was desperately trying to push the Hurricanes out and away from the front of the net.

Daylyn's slap shot came flying in low and hard, sailing through all the legs, skates, and pads to slide right through the goalie's five-hole.

Cheering erupted from the bench and the stands. Goal!

"Well done, Daylyn!" Georgia and Mia both shouted, slapping Daylyn on the back as they skated toward their bench.

"Thanks. Sorry about the penalty," she replied.

"If you hit the puck like that after a penalty, feel free to get a few more!" Millie said, hugging Daylyn and passing her a drink bottle as they traded places on the bench and watched the next line.

The Hurricanes were up 2-0. It was a great beginning to their finals run. So far, they'd been able to keep the Panthers' two fastest skaters to the outside of the ice. Without clear space, they hadn't been able to capitalize on their speed.

The siren sounded, signaling the end of the second period with the score at 2-0.

Then three minutes into the third period, the Panthers center took off with the puck after Aniyah fumbled on the blue line. Emma was backing Aniyah up but wasn't close enough to close the gap as the center blew through the gap.

So it was all up to Khloe, the Hurricanes' goalie.

The Panthers' center was closing in quickly on the Hurricanes' net as Khloe started slowly skating back toward her net, her eyes never leaving the girl flying toward her. Khloe knew the center liked to deke, so she anticipated the coming move.

Coach Phil had sat with Khloe during the afternoon while they waited, running through some of the highlight footage he had taken of one of the Panthers games. A little bit of practice and preparation could be key. If you understood how someone shoots and the moves they prefer, you'd be more prepared to anticipate where the pucks were going to come from.

Khloe kept repeating 1-2-3, 1-2-3, as she watched the girl skate toward her. It was as if time had stood still, and everything was moving in slow motion.

The Panther player faked to the left and then again to the right. Khloe knew the shot was coming any second. She stood in the middle of the net, never leaving her stance once during the fakes.

When the shot finally came, she was ready and zipped to her left, grabbing the puck easily in her glove. *It almost seemed too easy*, Khloe thought to herself. She took a sneaky look in her glove just to make sure the puck was there and hadn't snuck out and into the net.

The other girls came rushing in, congratulating Khloe with a rush of slaps, hugs, and fist bumps. It had been an incredible save. The Panthers' player angrily slapped her stick on the ice as she skated away disappointed.

That missed opportunity seemed to take the wind out of the Panthers' sails. For the rest of the game, the Hurricanes managed to keep them from scoring, with Mia managing to score another goal with only two minutes left on the board.

The Hurricanes ended their quarter-final game 3-0.

The boys' game was up next.

By the end of the first period, they were up 1-0. It was a tight game with both teams playing well, but it was apparent to everyone that both teams were lacking the legs they'd had earlier in the day. It was never easy playing three games in one day.

The shifts on both sides were getting shorter and shorter, with Coach John trying to give his players as much rest as possible.

The Dayton Dragons were getting rougher and rougher, but the referees just weren't calling the hits.

Tempers were up on the bench, and Coach John had to call a time out just to settle the boys down. Between the boys being sore from trips and slashing, everyone was tired and struggling.

The scores were still 1-0 for the Lightning after the end of the second period. The boys took as long as possible during the break, with the referees having to ask both teams to come back on the ice several times.

With five minutes left in the third period, the Dragons were able to get a quick goal after a scramble in front of the net. Logan tried his best to stop the puck, but with everyone crowding in on him, it was impossible to stop.

The scores were now tied 1-1 with three minutes left on the clock. No one wanted this game to go into overtime. They were all sore and exhausted.

Cameron, Hunter, and Luke were all back together on the same line and they were ready.

Cameron won the puck on the faceoff and flicked it back to Ben, who was quickly covered by the Dragons' winger. He sent the puck back into the corner, with both Cameron and Hunter desperately trying to recover the puck.

The Dragons' defense was slashing and hacking at the Lighting players' legs, doing whatever they could to try and get the puck. Despite the slashing, Cameron managed to come up with the puck and tried pushing it out of the group of players.

Unfortunately for Cameron, it didn't work, and he ended up tripped by one of the Dragons' defensive players. As he landed hard on the cold ice, he swiped at the puck desperately with his stick, sending it slowly sliding out in front of the net.

Luke swooped in, picking up the puck and flipping it over the goalie's head. Goal!

Everyone was cheering, with the score now 2-1, but the game wasn't over yet. There was still one minute left on the clock, and the Lighting were doing everything they could to desperately hold on to their lead.

Coach John sent out his strongest defensive line. They only had seconds left on the clock, but anything could happen in a hockey game.

The Dragons threw everything they had at the Lightning defense, but it wasn't enough to break through, and the final siren sounded, signaling the end of the game. The Lightning had done it! They'd taken the win in the quarter-final, finishing 2-1.

The celebrations were subdued, though, as the boys made their way off the ice. They were just too tired.

Luckily, the roads were now open, and everyone would be able to get a decent meal and a hot shower back at the hotel. The coaches had set another 8:30 p.m. curfew, but they knew most of the kids would be too tired to stay up much later anyway.

Millie was just getting out of the shower when she heard her phone chirping. It was a text from Liam telling her he'd won his game too and was about to leave the arena.

A few seconds later, another text came in from her coach, telling them all to eat in their rooms or with their parents and head straight to quiet time after that.

Millie lay down on her bed to text Liam back. She told him she was sad they wouldn't be able to hang out, but she was exhausted too, and she would be able to see him in the morning.

Liam texted her back saying goodnight, and Millie replied with the same. Only minutes later, she was drifting off to sleep, her eyes getting heavier by the second.

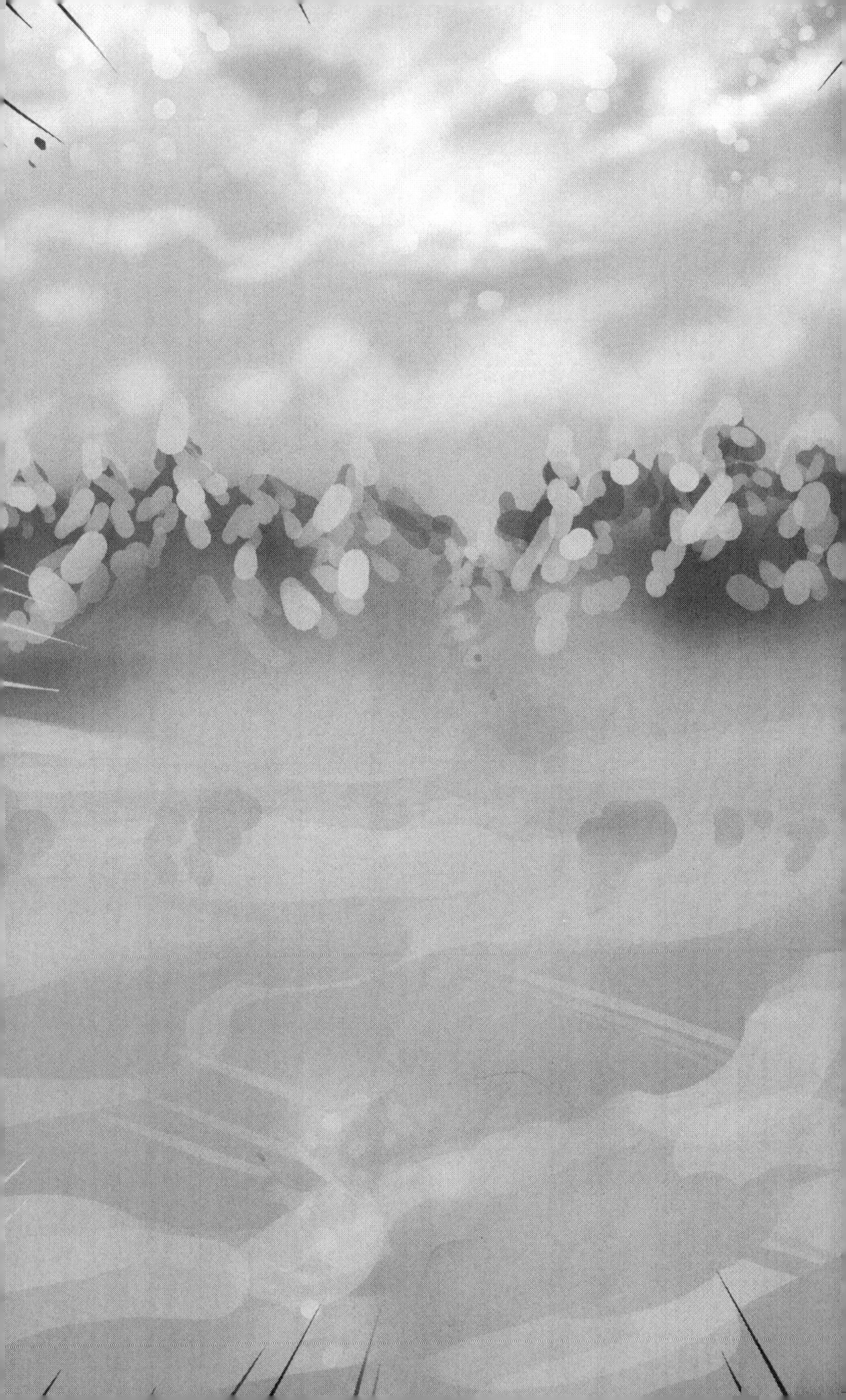

16

IT WAS THE last morning of the championships, and both the Dakota Lightning and Hurricanes were going into their semi-final games at the same time. The hotel dining room was packed full of excited and noisy kids, all starving and ready for a big day of hockey.

The boys had a huge battle ahead of them. They were playing the number one ranked team in the state: the Golden Hawks. The boys had managed to catch a little bit of their game the previous day, and what they'd seen was enough to worry them all.

The Hurricanes were playing the Branton Badgers in their semi-final game. The Badgers were close to the same rank as the Hurricanes, but they'd had a fantastic championship run so far.

The kids from both teams ate their food as quickly as possible. Their games were both at 8:00 a.m., and they had to be at the arena and ready well before then.

When they arrived at the arena, both coaches decided to let the teams warm up together. It wasn't often they both played at the same time in the same arena. It also allowed the coaches to chat and finish their coffees while the girls and boys all warmed up.

The girls and boys both had to do two complete circuits of the upstairs part of the arena. Usually, there would be a lot of horseplay and joking, but they were all focused on their upcoming games. When they finally got through the laps, they gathered around their coaches.

"Okay, everyone, listen up. Cameron and Millie have a few words to say before we all go off to our respective change rooms. So, pay attention. Go ahead, you two," Coach John yelled, getting everyone to stop their chatter mid-sentence and pay attention. As the two team captains, Cameron and Millie had decided they would do their pep talks together.

“Thanks, Coach John. We’re both going into two hard games, but whatever the outcome is, remember who you are,” Millie began. She didn’t enjoy public speaking, but it was different in front of all her hockey friends. “We’re here today to be the best we can be. Play your game, not theirs, and remember that no matter what, the outcome will be we did our best.”

“Thanks, Mills. She’s right, you know. We’re here not only representing our teams, but also our town. Let’s show them they breed them tough in Dakota! Now, three cheers for us!” Cameron shouted, leading the teams in three cheers.

“Dakota! Dakota! Dakota!” The kids all shouted together.

The girls were all nervously lined up on the ice, waiting to bump gloves with the Branton Badgers. The start of their semi-final game was only moments away from beginning.

The Hurricanes quickly got onto the board, scoring a goal after a mistake by the Badgers’ defense in front of their net. The Badgers were good, but the Hurricanes were better. If they kept playing with this level of intensity for the whole game, they should come out on top.

By the end of the second period, the Hurricanes were up 2-0 after a great shot from Daylyn from the post, with Mia gathering the rebound and putting the puck into the net. So far, Mia had been having an awesome championship weekend, and it was looking as if it would only get better.

The girls hit their bench with high spirits at the end of the second period.

“Okay, that was an awesome second period. You girls are doing great. I know it’s only the semi-finals, but I’m proud of each and every one of you. Now, Millie is going to say a few words. Drink some water and get ready for the last period!” Coach Phil said to the girls. He couldn’t wipe the smile off his face.

“Thanks, Coach! Now girls, listen to all those cheers. That’s our family and friends cheering out there for us. We’ve had a great game so far, so let’s get out there and finish this game as strongly as we started!” Millie shouted.

The third period was anticlimactic, with both teams failing to find the net again. However, it wasn’t for lack of trying. Khloe and the Badgers’ goalie were kept busy, and only their excellent skills in front of the net had prevented either team from scoring.

The Hurricanes had won their semi-final 2-0 over the Branton Badgers. They were going to the championship game!

On the other side of the rink, the Lightning boys weren't doing as well as the girls. They were down 2-0 heading into the third and final period of the game. Logan had been defending his net like he was possessed, but even his talent could only stop so many shots before some made it through.

They were struggling to keep up with the Golden Hawks, who were a physically much stronger team than them. The majority of the Lightning players were fast but small. While most of their team were seniors, they just didn't have the physical size of some of the other teams. Usually, in this situation, they could out skate their opponents, but it just wasn't happening today.

Not only were the Golden Hawks much bigger than the Lightning, but they were also fantastic skaters. They came from a much larger city, and the pool of players was much bigger than in Dakota. That meant getting onto the team was much more competitive and led to a higher caliber of player.

The first ten minutes of the third period had seen the Lightning mounting an increasingly defensive style of play because of the Golden Hawks' offensive pressure. It wasn't the way they usually played, and it was making it harder and harder for them to switch over and go on the defensive.

After a bad change by the Golden Hawks, Cameron finally saw his opportunity and grabbed the puck on a breakaway. It was now just him and the goalie, with no other players between them.

Cameron had watched this goalie play the day before and on some game tapes. He knew he was good, and Cam would have to make this shot count. As he was flying toward the goalie, he heard skates just behind him.

He skated hard and fast, directly at the goalie. He could see the top corner of the net over the goalie's shoulder and knew that's where he needed to aim the puck. The goalie was much stronger on his glove hand than his blocker, and the top corner was his weakest spot.

Cameron didn't hesitate a second longer. He took a wrist shot and watched the puck as it sailed over the outstretched goalie's blocker and hit the back of the net. Goal!

The score was now 1-2.

Cheers erupted from the stands surrounding the ice, and the Lightning players on the bench went ballistic. With only a few minutes left on the clock, they knew they needed to get another quick goal to even the score and push the game into overtime if they stood any chance of winning.

The Lightning gave it everything they had. Every line that went out on the ice gave 110%, coming back to the bench exhausted. They just couldn't catch a break.

It didn't matter if it was offense or defense, the Golden Hawks were amazing at either end of the ice. No one was getting anywhere close enough to get a good shot off on their net. With only a minute left on the clock, Coach John decided to give it one last push, sending out his best line.

The five seniors—Cameron, Luke, Preston, Ben, and Rhys—all headed out onto the ice for one last effort. They just couldn't do it. Not this time. Not this game.

The Golden Hawks had the puck in their end when the clock showed ten seconds remaining. They all started counting down the time. Cameron was trying hard to control his emotions as the buzzer sounded, signaling the end of the game. It was over.

Cameron looked around at his teammates; they all looked as devasted as he felt.

Meanwhile, at the other end of the ice, the Golden Hawks were celebrating with a giant dogpile, with all their players piling onto their poor goalie.

Cameron's eyes welled up with tears. He knew everyone was feeling just like him; it was just that some showed it more than others. As he slowly made his way off the ice toward the change room, he couldn't help but feel as though if only he'd tried a little harder, they might have won.

Once they were all in the change room, Coach John shut the door so it was just the coaching staff and the players in the room. "I'm so proud of you guys. You didn't win, but you played as a team, and you never gave up. We are the only team so far that's even scored on that team. You guys showed everyone you deserve to be here. It just wasn't meant to be our year. We'll be back next year better, bigger, and stronger." He paused and looked them all in the eye before continuing. "Cam wants to say a few words, so we'll give you guys five minutes alone. Well done."

Cameron still had tears in his eyes as he looked around at his teammates. "Guys, I know

how bad this feels right now, but I want you guys to know it's been a blast playing with you all this year. I didn't realize how much I could cry until that buzzer sounded." He paused for a second to gather himself together. "This hurts, sure. It's okay to be upset about losing, but don't blame yourself. We'll get them next time. Hopefully, the girls did better, and we can support them in the finals. Now, three cheers for the Lightning!"

"Lightning! Lightning! Lightning!" They all screamed as they banged their sticks on the ground.

There were mixed emotions as the boys and girls all met up. The girls were excited about winning but felt heartbroken for the boys. The Blue Devils had won their semi-final game too, so they would be playing the Golden Hawks in the championships later that day.

Liam, Cameron, and some of the other boys agreed to sit down with the Blue Devils so Cam could go through their game. Anything they could do to help the Blue Devils beat the Golden Hawks was okay with them.

17

WITH THE LIGHTNING out of the championships, it was now up to the Hurricanes to go through to the finals and try and take home the championship trophy. Liam and the Blue Devils had also been fortunate enough to make it through their semi-finals.

There was some time to kill before the championship games, so the Blue Devils' and Lightning coaches—plus Cameron, Liam, and some of the other Hurricanes boys—sat down to talk about the Golden Hawks. The Hurricanes usually wouldn't, but because the boys were friends and no one wanted to see the Golden Hawks win, they thought they'd make an exception.

The hockey talk was soon out of the way, and the boys left the coaches to chat while they went and hung out.

"I hope my arm's okay for lacrosse," Linkin said, waving his broken arm around in its large plaster cast. The cast was looking a little bit like a wall of graffiti with the whole hockey team having signed it.

"You all play lacrosse over the summer?" Liam asked.

"Um, yeah, most of us. Our trainer, Tyler, is an amazing lacrosse player. He used to play professional field and box lacrosse. He's organizing a new team this year to play in the Outlaw Lacrosse League. We all used to play in a league, but this new one is more of a tournament team. We usually struggle to get enough people in our area to play, so this works better as anyone can try out. So no, not all of us play, but a lot of us." Cameron replied.

"Does Millie play?" Liam asked, trying to make it sound casual but failing miserably, causing Cameron to laugh.

"Yep, her and most of the girls play. But they want to try out for this team this year. Some of them are really strong athletes, but it's different than girls' field lacrosse, so we're not sure how it will go. But it would make it a really great season if we all played together. Maybe you should try out? You're only an hour away from us, and we don't play regular-season games. We only play tournaments, so you're traveling anyway. Then you could hang out with Millie and the rest of us over summer."

"Sounds awesome. What's it called again? I'll get my mom and dad to check it out."

"Outlaw Lacrosse League," Cameron answered.

The rest of the conversation switched back and forth between hockey and lacrosse until Liam had to go and warm up for his game. *It was funny*, Cameron thought to himself. *Not too long ago, he'd hated Liam and the Blue Devils*. It had been Millie and Mia who had shown him it was one thing to be competitive on the ice, but off the ice, you could also be good friends.

"Good luck!" Cameron shouted to Liam and the rest of the Blue Devils as they headed off toward their change room.

"Thanks!" The boys shouted back.

The Hurricanes were playing against the Redding Rockets for the championship.

The Blue Devils' game was scheduled to start

an hour after theirs, so Liam and some of the other boys were watching the first period of the Hurricanes' game before running across to theirs.

Both the Rockets and Hurricanes were undefeated so far in the championships. The Rockets had come in at number one in the state.

There were a lot of nervous faces lined up near the door, which led out onto the ice. Millie and the rest of the girls had already talked in the change room about how they were the underdogs going into this game. Even though both teams were undefeated, the Rockets had some amazing players. The Rockets hadn't lost a game all weekend. Well, everyone would see how big the Hurricanes' bite could be!

The siren sounded, signaling the end of the previous game. So the games wouldn't run late, all the players were having photos taken and medal presentations done in the large press conference room next to the arena. The Hurricanes could get right onto the ice.

It was time for the Hurricanes to show everyone was a hockey team from Dakota could do!

The first period was a cautious back and forth between the Rockets and Hurricanes. Neither team wanted to try anything too risky, fearing if they turned over the puck, it would cost them.

They both spent their time feeling out their opposition, looking for weak spots. The first period ended with a score of 0-0.

Liam and the rest of the Blue Devils couldn't stay and watch any longer, and they headed off to their own game.

When the siren went at the end of the first period, Coach Phil pulled everyone into a huddle, not wasting a second. "Okay, you've had the first period to feel each other out. Now it's time to start taking a few risks out there. We aren't going to win playing safe. Now, get out there and push them. Push them harder than anyone else has ever pushed them. We can win this; we're the number one team in the state!"

The girls came out of the huddle with a new attitude and game plan. They knew they needed to stick to their strengths, playing their own offensive style and forgetting the defensive style they'd been playing in the first period.

After a whistle on Khloe, Coach Phil had decided it was time he switched up his lines. Mia, Millie, and Georgia were now playing on the same line together.

The girls were all lined up waiting for the referee to drop the puck, and Georgia was slowly moving backward away from the circle. The Rockets' winger was focused on the referee, and she hadn't noticed her player was no longer by her side.

Millie won the puck, passing it backward to Ashlyn. She glanced up and saw Georgia already heading up the ice toward the Rockets' defense.

The defense player was caught off guard, not expecting one of the Hurricanes' players to be bearing down on her all alone.

Ashlyn fired the puck perfectly through the pack of players, where it bounced off the boards and onto Georgia's stick.

Georgia didn't miss a beat. She was off and flying. It didn't hurt she was one of the fastest skaters on the Hurricanes' team but often went unnoticed due to her size. Georgia bore down on the goalie; it was one on one now.

The Rocket's goalie was tough—they wouldn't have gotten as far as they had if she wasn't a great goalie—but Georgia knew she often dropped out of her stance just a little earlier than she should. Georgia's plan was to fake low and then fire the puck in over the top.

Just like she planned, the goalie watched

Georgia's stick fly back like she was taking her shot, and as the stick started to swing forward, the goalie dropped low onto the ice. Georgia saw the goalie begin to drop and took the shot, sending the puck flying over the goalie's shoulder and into the net before she could react.

Goal!

Cheering erupted inside the arena, coming from everywhere. The Hurricanes' bench was filled with players hugging and banging their sticks on the boards.

"Okay, okay! Great job, but we've got a long way to go girls, so settle down and let's do it again. Make smart decisions and keep up the intensity out there!" Coach Phil said to the players on the bench and the girls skating out onto the ice to line up again.

The rest of the period saw neither team manage to get the puck in the net. There were some close calls, but excellent goaltending by the two goalies kept the score the same. It was 1-0 in the Hurricanes' favor going into the third and final period.

On the other side of the arena, things weren't going quite as well for the boys on the Blue Devils team.

They had started off strongly, quickly scoring a goal on the Golden Hawks in the first minute of the first period.

Their joy was short lived, however, as the Golden Hawks answered with a goal of their own, followed up a few minutes later with another one. It was 2-1 in favor of the Golden Hawks when the siren sounded at the end of the first period.

There was five minutes left in the third period when a rush toward Khloe in goal saw several girls from both teams landing awkwardly on her.

The referee blew her whistle. There was no goal, but Khloe wasn't getting back up. All the players on the ice took a knee while Tyler, the Hurricanes' trainer, rushed out to see if Khloe was okay.

Millie and Mia looked at each other with worried looks. They could hear Khloe crying while Tyler spoke to her quietly.

The Lightning boys were climbing all over to try to see what was happening out on the ice. As a goalie too, Logan wore a horrified look. He knew how easy it was to get hurt out there. Khloe was

also his best friend. The two of them walked home from school together every night.

Khloe slowly made her way to her feet, with Tyler helping her toward the Hurricanes' bench.

All the girls on the ice and the benches banged their sticks, and the audience was on their feet clapping. Khloe gave the Lightning boys a small wave, reassuring them she was okay.

Coach Phil got the referee's attention and called a time out. The Hurricanes didn't have a backup goalie, so they needed to give Khloe time to sit down and rest. The worst possible thing that could happen would be for her to be injured as one of the other players would need to fill in.

"I'm okay, Coach. I just need a few seconds. I seriously got the wind knocked out of me," Khloe said, taking a large drink from one of the water bottles.

"Are you sure, Khloe? That was a pretty big hit," Coach Phil asked, sounding concerned. Khloe was one tough girl, and it wasn't like her to get knocked down and not spring straight back up.

"Yeah. I'm okay. I've taken bigger hits from my older brother. I think I just landed weird on someone's knee or skate." Khloe slowly stood and started stretching, then grabbed her helmet as she stepped onto the ice. “No more dogpiles, please. I don’t think my back can carry you guys the whole game.”

The girls all laughed and gave her a fist bump as she slowly started skating toward her net. The other team started clapping, and so did the audience.

There were two minutes left on the clock when the Rockets pulled their goalie off the ice and sent another player out. They had put six of their strongest players on, and they looked like they meant business.

They quickly began to work the puck around, just waiting for the right opportunity to strike. The Hurricanes were trying to stick to their zones, but with that extra girl skating around on the ice, it was getting a bit sloppy.

Two of the Rockets’ players skated in front of the Hurricanes’ net and circled back in opposite directions. As the puck came to one girl, she must have seen her chance: she had a forward and her defense skating hard into the gap in the middle of the ice.

The Hurricanes saw what was happening but were just a few seconds behind.

The girl with the puck passed it to the defense

player skating toward the goal. The Rockets' defense player wound up her stick while their other players came in to pick up the rebound if there was one.

The Rockets' defense player connected cleanly with the puck, sending it flying toward Khloe. She saw it coming though and did a sliding save, sweeping her arm down with a textbook glove save.

While this was all happening, the clock had continued ticking down, and there were only fifteen seconds left of the third and final period.

Back at the face-off, all the girls were lined up in front. Every Hurricanes player needed to grab someone, so no one would get the opportunity to take a shot.

Mia took this faceoff as she had the best chance to win the puck and send it back to Ashlyn.

The referee dropped the puck, and both Mia and the girl from the Rockets battled for the puck, neither able to win in. A few players from both sides skated over to help.

Eventually, the puck got knocked to the boards and slid to a Rockets defense player who had a big shot open. Just as she went to wind up to take the shot, the buzzer sounded, and everyone rushed off the bench and raced over to Khloe. The Hurricanes had won the championship!

The girls all started throwing their gloves and helmets in the air, hugging each other and crying. Both teams were called to the conference room to get their medals.

The Rockets hung their heads low, and some of the girls were in tears, but not for the same reason as the Hurricanes. Each of the Rockets solemnly went up to get their silver medal as their names were called.

Once they were done, the Hurricanes were called up one by one to get their gold medal before Millie—as the captain—and Coach Phil were called up to get their championship trophy. Both teams posed for photos with their medals before breaking into smaller groups.

Several of the Rockets' players shook hands and congratulated the Hurricanes and vice versa. The Rockets' goalie made her way over to Khloe, who was posing for photos with Mia and Millie.

"Um, hey. Sorry to interrupt. I just wanted to say you had a great game."

"Oh, wow. Thanks! You too," Khloe replied, giving the other girl a fist bump.

The Blue Devils had managed to keep the Golden Hawks from scoring during the second period, but they were running on fumes as the boys headed into the third period of their championship game on the other side of the arena.

It was midway through the third period when things started to go seriously wrong for the boys of the Blue Devils. Their defense was the more exhausted of the two teams, with their coach already rotating his forwards into defense for short lines and changes to try and rest them as much as possible.

The Golden Hawks meanwhile looked fresh and were applying intense pressure on the Blue Devils. With five minutes left on the clock, the Golden Hawks put another puck in the net, which took the score to 3-1.

It was the end of the Blue Devils' championships. The final score was 3-1, with the Golden Hawks going through as undefeated champions.

18

COACH PHIL, COACH John, and the other staff got both teams together in another large meeting room at the arena once they'd all finished taking their photos. It was their last opportunity to speak to all the kids together before tryouts for next season.

"Okay, okay, everyone settle down. I know you're all excited, and we won't keep you too long. I know your parents are looking forward to getting on the road and getting home," Coach John said, getting a laugh from all the parents and some of the kids. "All the other coaches and I just wanted to say thank you to all of you for the hard work you put in this season and this weekend."

"That's right. You have all been amazing to coach again this year, and I'm looking forward

to coaching you again next year. Now, before you go, remember that hockey tryouts for next season start in a few weeks. We're going to have three tryout days spread out to give everyone equal opportunity to make it," Coach Phil added.

"So, don't forget, or you'll miss out!" Coach John shouted, startling a few of the kids in the front row.

"He's so loud," Khloe whispered to Rhys, who was sitting next to her.

"He has really good hearing—" Rhys began before Coach John interrupted.

"Pardon, Rhys? I have good what?"

"Good teeth, Coach John. I was just telling Khloe how nice your teeth are," Rhys said quickly. Khloe giggled beside him.

"Thanks, I think. Now, our lovely trainer, Tyler, has a few words to say, and then you're all free to get out of here."

"Thanks, John, Phil. Okay everyone, this will only take a few minutes more, and then you can go. As some of you know, we're doing lacrosse again this year. We're entering a team in the Outlaw Lacrosse League. It's a bit of a different setup, so it will involve traveling to various parts of the state to compete. Usually only one-day events. Practices will only be held on off weekends. Tryouts will be in a few weeks. If anyone is interested in trying out, let me know after the meeting, and I'll email your parents all the details. This is a coed league, so anyone can tryout, but it will follow regular field lacrosse rules. So, any girls playing will need to get new field helmets and sticks, but we would love to see some girls come out to play. That's it from me. I'm looking forward to seeing you at both the lacrosse and hockey tryouts. Great job!"

A few of the parents were rubbing their heads as if they'd suddenly developed migraines. Just when they thought they'd get a few weekends off, something else came along. *Oh well*, was the pervasive thought. *At least it beat having their kids sitting around on consoles all day.*

The kids, on the other hand, were chattering and talking excitedly amongst themselves about the upcoming lacrosse team and who was trying out for it.

It was time to put away the skates and get the lacrosse sticks out for the boys and girls of the Dakota Hurricanes and Lightning!

The End

HOCKEY WARS 5
LACROSSE WARS

COMING SPRING 2020

Made in the USA
San Bernardino, CA
26 January 2020